Davy Jones

& the Heart of Darkness

Includes an appendix with two essays from

"The Cave of Cinema Dave"

By Dave Montalbano

With illustrations by Rachel Galvin

DEDICATION

This novella and two essays are dedicated to all the United States of America Military Veterans who confronted *the Heart of Darkness*. Instead of being consumed by *the Heart of Darkness,* these individuals went on to create some wonderful and fun loving families.

Jerome S. Montalbano	U.S. Army	World War II
Dave G. Watson	U.S. Army	World War I
Herman Watson	U.S. Army	World War II
DeWitt Watson	U.S Air Force	Korea
William Watson	U.S. Army	
Frankie Mendolia	U.S. Navy	
Carmine "Junie" Mendolia	U.S. Navy	
Eddie Rydowski	U.S. Navy	
Emanual "Buddy" Pace	U.S. Navy	
Dominic Marzigliano	U.S. Army	

CONTENTS

Davy Jones & the Heart of Darkness

ACKNOWLEDGMENTS

Written during the Lenten Season of 2009, *Davy Jones & the Heart of Darkness* was blessed with many positive influences.

Fairy Godmother Sheryl Appelbaum was the first person to decode my handwriting. She provided great feedback.

Besides her final edit, Cinema Dave is thankful to Rachel Galvin for her illustrations that captured the spirit and tone of this novella.

Photographer extraordinaire Barbara McCormick for taking our glamour shot during an ugly time. Barbara is the hidden treasure of Palm Beach!

Staples representative Brenton Gaskill for his graphics support, together we built this book cover!

Besides providing my Dad much inspiration in his final 16 years, the Ship Modelers Club of South Florida reminded me about the importance of having a hobby during good times and bad. In particular, Cinema Dave acknowledges the kind words of Howard Brown, Bob Goldstein, Shelly Goldstein, David Goldstein, Frank Johnson, Admiral Stan Kemper, Fred Massimilla, Ralph Piera, Rudy Rigo, Jerry Urtnowski and Bob Werner. Dad's tools are now under the Ship Modelers Club's stewardship.

Through the years, the following people have helped navigate Cinema Dave through the Heart of Darkness:

All my Montalbano and Watson families, cousins and in-laws. Troy Adams, Adventurer's Club cast & crew, Cathy Anthony with the Doreen Gauthier Lighthouse Point Library, Joan Baker, Tony Barbieri, Ray Brasted and "Paparazzi Girl," Kevin Card, Bob Carter, Gerry Carter, CJ's Comics, Jeff Crevier, Alyn Darnay, Ward & Patty Donoho, Stan "Davis," Entre Nu, Anthony Espina, John Farese, Lesia Faulkner-Watson, Michelle Giedraitis-Botelho, Family of "Bailee Madison," Karen Ann and Steve Hunter, Ellen Jaffe, Blaine, Bruce, Jo & Mary Kimball, David Kirby and Barbara Hamby, Pat Larkin-Farrow, Mary Leone, Michael McCarthy, Al McGhee, Marianne Maylath, Carol Marshall, Woody Meckes, James McNalis, Jan Mitchell & Associates, Emily Neighbors, Anita Nelson, Chris Noel, Observer staff, Kelly Palmer-Skidmore, Jessica and Jose Prendes, Lena Putzer, Linnea Quigley, Andrew Sigman, Lynn Spinella-Pagans, Beverley Randolph, Bryce Rumbles, Bonnie Shafer-VanAlphen, Peter Wein, Claudia Wells, Arlene Wicks-Allen, Elaine Viets and Don Crinklaw.

Dave Montalbano

Captain's Prologue

*C*aptain Davy Jones leaned over his pipe organ, too drained to play his

dirge. He looked upon a closed musical locket.

He shouted, "No!"

He bellowed and swept the locket off the pipe organ with his claw-like left arm. His life was forever ruined the moment he laid his eyes upon her. She, and she alone, turned him into the monster that he had become.

Inspired, Davy Jones plunged his tentacle beard upon the basso profundo keys of the pipe organ. The crew of the Flying Dutchman felt secure when their captain played his music. The crew worked and performed their tasks at a quicker speed. The sailors did their job to perfection, for they did not want to feel the wrath of the cat of nine tails from Tobey, the Bo 'sun. Tobey was the quintessential Bo 'sun or Boatswain, the captain's mate who prided himself by searing flesh from the bones of those who did not heed the captain's orders.

As written by Morgan and Bartholomew, the Pirate's Code forbade the playing of music on the Sabbath. Davy Jones disregarded this particular code, which he saw mostly as a guideline. No one was his master. When the mood hit him, Davy Jones would play his pipe organ at any time and any place.

Captain Davy Jones kept himself separated from the crew. The captain of the Flying Dutchman seemed to have a closer relationship with the Kraken, a frightful but dumb beastie that sent many a sailor to Davy Jones' locker. Captain Davy Jones was an intelligent man, educated in the lore of the sea, the mechanics of sailing and marlinspike. Perhaps Davy Jones saw the Kraken as an extension of himself. The giant squid was 700 times the size of his master. As the Kraken's *tentacles could reach for things at distance, the Kraken extended the reach of Davy Jones.*

Davy Jones wanted what the Kraken had, no feelings and no emotions. When the Kraken sank a ship and digested the crew, the need was primal, not basic. The Kraken was the last of its kind. The Kraken had no mate. Davy Jones envied this aspect of the beastie; this creature never knew how lonely it was.

Davy Jones growled. Everything in the captain's cabin reminded him of her. Damn her. He rose from the bench and stumped his way to the location of the locket. As he leaned over to pick it up, his Bo 'Sun knocked on the cabin door.

"Captain! Message from the Admiral," Bo 'Sun Tobey shouted.

Davy Jones closed his eyes, his beard of tentacles shook. Davy Jones clutched the locket and shut his eyes. I am dammed to all eternity because of that woman. Hang the admiral and his navy, I am Davy Jones!

Davy Jones placed the locket on the pipe organ and exited the cabin. The sun was setting and Davy Jones kept a watchful eye for the green flash. It was his charge that he perform the chores of Old Charon, to ferry the souls of the dead to the next world. Davy Jones had gotten lax in this task and the living dead now corrupted the daily lives of the living.

The smaller sailing vessel was tethered alongside the Flying Dutchman. As a matter of protocol, four armed guards exited the H.M.S. Jaggerty. The captain of the H.M.S. Jaggerty boarded the Flying Dutchman with the arrogance of a sailor of the empire.

"Captain Jones, I presume?" the prim bald officer with the horseshoe haircut asked.

"And who might the captain of the Flying Dutchman be speaking to?" Davy Jones countered.

The captain of the H.M.S. Jaggerty seemed taken aback by this lack of protocol. This lack of protocol was more offensive to the captain of the H.M.S. Jaggerty than the fish faced crew of the Flying Dutchman.

He said, "I am Captain Sydney with direct correspondence from our Royal Admiral."

Davy Jones rolled his eyes in annoyance.

Captain Sydney continued, "The Admiral has asked that you euthanize the sea beast known as Kraken."

The crew of the Flying Dutchman laughed a hearty laugh. Captain Sydney glared with disdain at the Captain of the Flying Dutchman. The Captain of the H.M.S. Jaggerty presented the parchment to Davy Jones. Captain Davy Jones grabbed the parchment with his slimey right hand. After reading the words, Davy Jones handed the parchment to his Bo 'Sun and stared at the diffident Captain Sydney.

Davy Jones turned to Tobey and said, "We all know what this means."

The cannons roared. The wood of the H.M.S. Jaggerty splintered and rose to the sky. The smell of sulfur filled the air.

The surviving sailors of the H.M.S. Jaggerty swam towards the Flying Dutchman. Davy Jones sniffed at the smoke in the air and some ash fell upon his beard of tentacles.

"The Admiral shall hear of this!" Captain Sydney screamed.

"Captain Sydney, do you fear death?" Davy Jones asked.

"I fear the wrath of the Admiral more than your melodramatic pronouncements!"
Captain Sydney screamed.

"Bold talk from the Captain of a sinking ship.
A captain who should have gone down with the ship,"
Davy Jones said with a smile.

Captain Sydney knew the lore of Davy Jones better than the other previous
captains caught in the lair of Davy Jones Locker. Davy Jones sensed this about
Captain Sydney. The captain of H.M.S. Jaggerty did not fear death, not on this day.

As he scanned the debris in the ocean, Davy Jones noticed a curly-headed young
man swimming with a plank in front of him. On the plank was a wicker bird cage
with a parrot inside. The parrot's feathers were ruffled. Captain Davy Jones was
mesmerized by this sailor, who was caring for his pet.

The bird cage first boarded the Flying Dutchman, followed by bare feet, muscular
legs of a dark curly headed teenager. As the tall teenager put both bare feet on the
deck of the Flying Dutchman, he turned and saw the aquamarine crew of the Flying
Dutchman for the first time.

The young man spoke,
"Sbagliato! Momma mia!"

Davy Jones looked upon this tall creature with his ripped pants and ruffled shirt.
He carried this wicker cage of a nervous bird. The young man was marked for
death, but Davy Jones sensed that this was a mistake. In his many years since
accepting the chores of Charon, it was rare that a soul fated for doom seemed so
full of life.

Captain Sydney seemed annoyed by the curly-headed sailor.

"Cabin boy," Captain Sydney spoke with his sneer of cold contempt, "I am conveying orders to the Captain of the Flying Dutchman. I would appreciate that you not become such a spectacle at this moment!"

Davy Jones was bored with the pompous courier from the Admiral. The Cabin Boy, named Pasquale Montalban, looked like a simpleton angel. Captain Sydney continued to speak, but Davy Jones ignored him. The captain of the Flying Dutchman limped to Pasquale Montalban.

The parrot started to flutter and squawk. Davy Jones looked at the bird and then at Pasquale. Pasquale was taller than he, so the captain of the Flying Dutchman had to look up to his captive. This situation took Davy Jones off his stride, much like a certain sea captain who Davy Jones recently fed to the Kraken.

"Your bird fears death, do you?" Davy Jones asked.

Pasquale looked at Davy Jones in puzzlement. Perhaps it was a language barrier or perhaps it was the roar of the cannons that dumbed his hearing.

Pasquale just smiled and said, "Come se dice?"

"Come se dice?" Davy Jones repeated, "What did I say you asked??? On the Flying Dutchman, we speak the royal language of English; can you speak the lord's tongue?"

Pasquale recognized two words from Davy Jones' lips;
"Royal" and "Lord."

Pasquale reached into his shirt and produced a wooden cross.
Davy Jones had seen many a dying soldier clutch their idols of worship in their final moments. Many pleaded for more time to set things right in their lives. It seemed as if Pasquale was offering the cross as a gift.

Despite the many years of ferrying souls to the afterlife, Davy Jones never encountered a creature like this Pasquale. Davy Jones was taken aback by this silent gesture. As he stepped backwards, the parrot settled on the perch in the wicker bird cage. Pasquale smiled as he removed the cross from his neck.
"To you con grazie, with thanks," he said.

Davy Jones was truly befuddled by this innocent. Pasquale was not like the disciplined crew under Captain Sydney's command. The boy must have thought he was being rescued by the crew of the Flying Dutchman.

Davy prepared to send Pasquale to the brig when Captain Sydney spoke,
"Now Jones, as you have control of the seas, the Admiral has control of you. Therefore, you will follow his orders. Instead,

you have disobeyed orders and sank one of your Admiral's ships. The Admiral will provide punishment upon you!"

Davy Jones looked at Captain Sydney and then at the caged bird.

"Then I have nothing to lose," Davy Jones reasoned, "Bo 'Sun, escort Captain Sydney and the survivors of the H.M.S. Jaggerty to the brig -"

Davy turned to his Bo 'Sun, "Please escort Pasquale Montalban and his bird to my cabin."

Bewildered, Pasquale followed Bo 'Sun Tobey to the captain's cabin. Captain Sydney's face simmered. Captain Davy Jones was not following protocol of the Admiral. A captain of the Admiral's fleet should not be imprisoned with the common soldiers and sailors, especially, when a slow-witted cabin boy was treated like royalty. Captain Sydney whispered that the Admiral would hear of Davy Jones' breach of protocol.

Davy entered the captain's quarters and saw Pasquale standing over the pipe organ. The lad looked like he wanted to play the instrument, but was obedient enough not to press the keys until he secured permission.

It was when the parrot squawked that Pasquale realized Captain Davy Jones was standing squarely in the room. Davy was used to intimidating the people in his private cabin, but Pasquale seemed unfazed. Davy needed to know why this doomed sailor seemed not to fear him.

Captain Davy Jones began talking to his captive in the Italian language. Davy Jones was the master of many languages, a skill he learned from the ghost of Nimrod, the master builder from the tower of Babel. Davy Jones often hailed Nimrod when the Flying Dutchman neared the gates of the afterlife. Through the magic of communication, Davy and Pasquale conversed in one language.

"As I asked you before, do you fear death?" Davy asked.

*"I fear not seeing my Beatrix again, but I do not fear death,"
Pasquale replied and he touched the crucifix around his neck.*

*Davy Jones winced; he had not seen this Christian hero when circumnavigating the
Seven Seas. Charon claimed to have rowed a carpenter from Galilee into the next
world. Given Charon's questionable character, Davy wondered if this Jesus person
actually existed.*

*Unlike most of his captors, Pasquale seemed incredibly comfortable with his
destiny. Most people clutch their religious idolatry and pray loudly. Mostly, Davy
was able to recruit crew mates to serve 100 years on the Flying Dutchman because
of their fear of dying. It was rare that sailors did not take Davy's option to serve,
but Davy had been noticing that recent people had chosen certain death rather than
serve 100 years aboard the Dutchman.*

"Tell me who this Beatrix is," Davy asked.

*"I wait so long to see my Beatrix. Now I have to wait longer. Beatrix and I will be
together. That is our destiny and the wait hurts, but Beatrix and I will endure,"
Pasquale replied.*

*"You are a FOOL," Davy Jones roared at Pasquale,
"Love is a bond that is easily severed; you are a fool to wait for a woman!"*

*Pasquale said, "So I have been told by people who have never met my Beatrix, but
that is not our destiny."*

*Davy Jones continued, "Foolishness is the price of youth. This foolishness will
pass and you will learn that a man is only measured by his actions in this world and
the next."*

Pasquale said, "If the actions you choose are good, then you will live a good life. You choose badly, and then you live badly.

Davy Jones said,
"You are naive. Young man, let me educate you. There is neither good nor bad. There are merely shades of grey."

Pasquale said, "This sounds like the argument of somebody who avoiding the responsibility of suffering."

Davy Jones bellowed,
"You think you can lecture me on morality? What do you know about life in your puny years compared to my years on the Flying Dutchman?"

Pasquale said in a soft voice, "I know I am happier than you."

Davy Jones said, "Ignorance is bliss."

Pasquale said, "Not if the ignorance is chosen."

Davy said,
"Chosen ignorance, boy you must be daft. What one pretends not to know is more destructive than natural ignorance."

"That is something I will consider, Captain Jones, when I run for political office," Pasquale said.

Jones was surprised that Pasquale considered his point of view.

"I see I have a philosopher in the captain's cabin. I salute you," Captain Davy Jones replied.

Davy slightly bowed his head and made a twirling motion with his right hand, his tentacle fingers flipping in the air.

Pasquale said, "Grazie, Il Capitano, I was raised in Florence, where one breathes philosophy as one drinks water. Some of the great minds were grown in Florence, the birth place of my language. Dante Alighieri, Leonardo Da Vinci, Michelangelo Buonarroti, Niccole Machiavelli … all great minds, all driven to be unhappy."

Davy commented,
"Those are names that will last for all eternity, individuals who sold their souls for eternal life. You claim to be a Christian and Christians pursue the same goals."

Pasquale said, "Christians begin to live eternal life when they accept Jesus. Accepting Jesus is not quid pro quo; Jesus is acceptance, understanding and love."

The word "Love" was an obscenity for Davy's ears. The tentacles on his beard bristled. At this moment, he wanted to thrash this Florentine and feed him to the Kraken.

Davy Jones said,
"Love is one of the great illusions perpetuated between man and God. Love is the peace treaty between Lucifer and God, to amuse the devils and angels. The devil does not understand love; if so, he would remain in paradise. I have been of this world a long time, but I was not there when Satan and God had their argument. I do know that God threw Satan out of Heaven. If God was passionate, God would have not created this separation from his most beautiful angel."

Pasquale replied,
"This most beautiful angel only thought of his own beauty, not the beauty of the actions of others."

"Selfish people take the good deeds in others and provide nothing in return," Davy countered.

"We are talking angels, devils and theology. Your last comment sounds like something of a personal comment," Pasquale replied.

Davy Jones said, "Perceptive boy, why are you here?"

Pasquale wanted to remind Davy Jones that he invited him here, but he felt as if the captain of the Dutchman wanted to know more about his life.

Pasquale began his biography,
"I am from Florence, on the Italian peninsula. My family died when I was young and I was raised by the Holy Order of Santa Cruces. I was expelled from the order, but I was grateful for the knowledge that I obtained. I managed to pick up work as a carpenter and a brick layer. Beatrix would pass on the streets and I would smile. She was an angel and did not seem to belong to the Royal bloodline of the Pazzi family."

"Ah yes, I ferried a few souls from the Pazzi conspiracy. Many Florentines were thrown into the Arno River, much bloodshed," Davy Jones interrupted.

Pasquale continued,
"Like me, Beatrix lost her parents in her youth. She was adopted by the Pazzi family. Despite their best intentions, Beatrix was a square cog in a circular machine. As beautiful as Beatrix is, she did not have the royal aptitude. She wore the wrong colors at the wrong time. She preferred to walk in the fields and sing to the sheep, lamb and cows. We sang together in the Boboli gardens and we would meet every Sunday afternoon."

Davy Jones rolled his eyes.

Pasquale blushed as he continued his story,
"As beautiful as Florence is, we both knew our destinies lay elsewhere. With Lira that we both had saved, we eloped and traveled the peninsula. Through her

singing, Beatrix joined a traveling theatre guild. Given my background in the arts and construction, I stage managed. We were always poor, but happy."

Pasquale stopped for moment and slowly continued, "We were to have a child, but she miscarried early."

Pasquale paused and made the sign of the cross.

"We both realized that if God planned to bless us with children, we needed a more stable life. We heard of the new country. Beatrix had cousins that live in the New York City state, so I gave her my money so she could settle there. I would join her and we could both start our new life," he said.

"What if your precious Beatrix is not on the dock waiting for her long lost stone builder?" Davy Jones asked.

"Then, she will be in the kitchen cooking our first dinner," Pasquale smiled.

Davy Jones looked at him incredulously, "You think so?"

Pasquale stated with determination, "I know so."
Davy Jones said, "So certain is youth, so doubtful is experience."
Pasquale asked, "Did someone not wait for you?"

Davy Jones roared. With his left claw Davy Jones slammed his dining table. The table split through the table top and legs. The parrot squawked. Davy Jones bellowed, "Bo'Sun! Take this neophyte and his bird to the brig!"

Pasquale and his parrot followed the Bo'Sun out of the Captain's cabin. Davy Jones flung his arms into the air in frustration. He quickly limped to the dining table, broke off a leg and began smashing the table.

After turning his Captain's table into kindling, Davy Jones staggered to his pipe organ. For an immortal being, Davy Jones was amazed at how he could physically exhaust himself.

Yet, his mind would not rest; how dare this infidel asks HIM, the captain of the Flying Dutchman, such questions.

Davy Jones sarcastically repeated Pasquale's comment,
"DID SOMEONE NOT WAIT FOR YOU AT THE DOCK?"

Davy Jones plunged his tentacle shaped beard upon the keyboard. With ferocity, Davy Jones lost his mind to the bassoon profundo dirge that he was playing.

Captain's Log

I
His Young Years

When a child is born, the lass or laddie has no concept of how rich or impoverished they might be. Davy Jones was born in Scotland to a clan that claimed to have fought with William Wallace. Much of this folklore could not be proven, but little Davy Jones did witness unity between Ireland and Scotland with the arrival of Columba the Monk. Columba eventually became the patron saint for bookbinders.

While literacy was not a priority for the Jones family, Davy took an interest in books. Davy noted every day rituals of the clan and recorded dates, times and techniques of warfare. He took time to witness the types of sheep and the grass where the sheep grazed. The childhood of Davy Jones was landlocked, but the lad was easily distracted by all forms of water; rivers, lakes and streams.

Much like Pasquale Montalban, Davy grew up without parents. It was not until he began to ferry the souls to the underworld that he learned that his parents died of a combination of malnutrition and disease. The young Davy Jones was raised by the Jones Clan as if he were community property. The orphan had his uses; Davy was one of the best sheep herders and animal wranglers on the isle.

As Davy matured, he learned that people could be duplicitous and mean spirited. He also noticed that animals did not have this trait. If an animal growled; it was for a good reason. The growl meant that something was intruding. A trickster human might not warn the intruder with the courtesy of a growl. The trickster would wait for the opportune moment and knife the intruder in the back of the head.

Davy appreciated the honest nature of the animals he protected. He felt regretful when a lamb would be slaughtered for a meal. As he grew out of adolescence, Davy had to perform this arduous task himself. The young butcher would cry.

Davy would survey the banquet hall and watch the drunken festivities. It upset him that so many slaughtered animals would be wasted on the gluttons in the hall. Davy vowed that if he became the leader of men, he would not allow such waste of life and flesh.

The concept of ritual sacrifice to the gods was baffling to Davy. He did not understand why animals would be herded into a gigantic wicker statue to appease the pagan gods of the soil. After the animals were put into their cages, music was played and people sang in chorus. Then the wicker man was set afire and the animals were burned alive. The screams of slaughter gave Davy Jones a lifetime of nightmares.

This was considered a religious ceremony, but young Davy could not comprehend this contemptible act; he could not understand why humans were so cruel to another living being. Davy reasoned that the gods behind the ritual of animal sacrifice were a bunch of deluded clansmen who drank strong mead. Witnessing these actions, Davy Jones became an atheist.

By not contributing to the community festivities, Davy became a social outcast. When his chores were completed, the young Davy would walk along the countryside by the rivers and streams in the valley. As the community prepared for another festival with the wicker sacrifice, Davy went for a long walk to get away from the noise and smell. The further Davy walked away from his clan, the more silent the cries of animal sacrifice became.

For a boy that never walked more than five miles from his clan, Davy felt reborn seeing the new countryside. Davy heard the sounds of the ocean before he saw the shore. He saw his first fish, which swam towards the opening of the inlet. He walked to the top of a natural barrier and looked upon his first beach. There were white caps and the wind was chilly. For the first time in his life, an ocean mist dampened Davy's forehead.

For the first time in this short portion of his life, Davy felt he was where he belonged.

II
His First Job

Davy lost all track of time; he was transfixed by the endless bowl of water. Night did fall and he sniffed the smoke of food. He followed the scent to a tavern on the shore.

The tavern was a very loud place with rowdy patrons. With hat in hand, Davy offered to do chores for food or drink. The bartender eyed this raggedly country boy with suspicion.

A man sitting at the bar said, "C'mon, Angus, hire this kid. Maybe we can get some hot food before the mayor outlaws fire."

Angus the bartender looked at his regular patron with mock disdain. Angus then looked back at Davy and began to ladle some soup for the hungry young man.

Angus spoke, "You are not good to me if you are weak. Eat this food and you can help me close down this place of undesirables."

Angus looked at the patron with a *see-I-told-you-so* expression. The patron gestured to Angus for more free grog. Angus made a sarcastic face. The patron said, "It is not for me, it is for your business partner."

Davy looked at the red-haired ruddy looking man. Davy felt gratitude, but he also was suspicious of his new acquaintance's motives. The patron many have sensed this, so he reached out his right hand.

The patron said, "Me name is Jonah, what is your name?"

"Davy Jones," Davy replied as he reached out his right arm to return Jonah's handshake.

"Mighty glad to meet you Master Jones," he said. "You tell me if this Angus tries to charge you for this meal, minus the agreement you two made about agreeing to work with him tonight. Now take a swig of this!"

Jonah put a goblet of hot buttered rum up to Davy Jones mouth. The warmth of the brew made Davy feel warm from his head to his toes. He finished the grog and began licking his lips. He was too poor to ask for more grog, so he did not ask for a refill.

Potatoes and fish were served. The odor on this plate was completely different. It smelled fresh. It was the first time Davy had tasted fish. He loved how flaky this food was compared to the tough chew of hare or squirrel. Davy ate every morsel of food. Satiated, Davy Jones surveyed the pub patrons.

There were many activities at the local tavern. There was the dart competition and the lusty wenches trying to seduce money out of the local politicians.

The nightlife was settled by a few songs, with an occasional chorus and responses. Davy felt out of place, he was not familiar with any of these tunes, but by the end of the evening, Davy joined in voice.

The lusty wenches and their paramours were the first to leave the tavern.

Jonah turned to Davy and said, "Now, you are going to earn your keep."

Davy nodded in understanding.

Davy looked at Angus, who was extinguishing candles and removing the tavern's eating utensils. The interior of the tavern was becoming dark. One group of three rowdies were talking over each other at the same time, no one was listening to what the other was saying.

Angus told Davy, "Get them to leave."

Davy rose from his stool and slowly approached the table of the rowdies. Jonah winked at Angus, behind Davy's back.

The rowdies stopped their nonsensical talk and observed the tall, thin apprentice boy of Angus. The rowdies knew it was the end of the evening. The rowdies just didn't know how many black and blue marks this bouncer was going to get.

Davy leaned forward and placed his hands on two chairs.

"Gentleman, you know why I am here. Angus wants you to go home," Davy said.

"Oh, Angus lets us stay here. Your job is to keep the fire going and bring us some more hot buttered grog," the hook-nosed rowdy said.

Davy smiled and looked back at Angus and Jonah, who offered no assistance. Davy's hands kept contact with the chairs.

"See that is not what Angus told me. In fact -" Davy said, leaning closer to the rotten smelling rowdies, " - in fact, Angus said that the people at this table would do something to hurt me."

Of course, Angus did not say this to Davy, but Davy knew that he was being tested.

The fat rowdy jumped out of his chair like a charging bull. Davy picked up the chair with his left hand. The fat rowdy stopped. The red-headed rowdy launched at Davy's knees. Davy stepped aside and smashed the chair over the red-haired rowdy's head. The chair broke. The red-headed rowdy collapsed face first upon the floor.

The hook-nosed rowdy threw a burning candle at Davy. While some wax spattered on Davy's stomach, he managed to swat the candle with the chair in his right hand. The candle flew back to the fat rowdy's big belly. The candle flame ignited his beard. The fat rowdy began to roar in fear, while his rowdy compatriots began pointing at him and laughing.

From behind the bar, Angus and Jonah observed the spectacle of this young man. From the low candlelight, both Angus and Jonah noticed the four legs from the broken chair emanating from Davy's arms. As a shadow on the wall, the chair legs looked attached to him, as if he had eight arms.

Davy feared for the fat rowdy with the flaming beard. He dropped the chair in his right hand, grabbed a pitcher of watered grog and threw the liquid on the rowdy's face and chest. The flames extinguished.

The fat rowdy stood up and patted his face. Fortunately, for the rowdy fat one, Davy's reaction time was so swift, that only his beard and some chest hair were burned off.

The hook-nosed and red-headed rowdy were still laughing at their mate. The fat rowdy calmed himself for a few seconds. He looked at his partners who howled with drunken laughter. The fat rowdy looked at Davy and gave him a gentle nod.

The fat rowdy then put his hands on the side of his partner's heads. Within a moment, he crashed their heads together. The laughter stopped. The fat rowdy staggered out of the tavern. The red-headed rowdy and his hooked nose companion followed, both rubbing the sides of their heads.

Jonah bellowed out, "Mighty impressive, for a young man. You really took care of yourself. Where did you say you were from?"

As he began cleaning up, Davy explained to Jonah about life in the wild country. Davy told Angus about his experiences with nature, animals and sheep herding.

"You handled the Buckner Clan pretty easily. Angus always sent his new recruits to kick the Buckner cousins out. We had some laughs in the past, always at the new recruit's expense."

Jonah stopped himself and looked away, a smile broadened across his wrinkly face. He looked at Davy and said, "Lad, I sense a wonderful destiny, but in the meantime, let me escort you to slumber."

Davy said, "Cannot go yet. I must help Angus clean up."

Angus bellowed, as he was bolted the door, "You already did, laddie. By kicking the Buckner cousins out, you cleaned out the scum. Have a good night."

III
His Vision

Davy's place of slumber consisted of a bed inside the room of a windmill. The room cracked and the windmill squeaked, but Davy was tired and slept.

The sun's rays beamed upon his face. He awoke and sat straight up. He looked up and could not remember if had ever slept under a roof before.

Davy dressed and went for a walk in the village. The baker was the first tradesman awake. The aroma of baking bread was the sweetest odor that Davy had ever sensed. Davy located the ocean and breathed in the salty air. He did not know why he left the safety of his clan, but he knew that he belonged to the sea.

He walked along the shore and away from civilization. He was used to jagged rocks and green grass; he was not used seeing wet jagged rocks and ocean's white foam. Davy lost track of time and the civilization of Angus, Jonah and the Buckner cousins.

Davy noticed a large unusual brown rock a few leagues out in the ocean. The rock was unusual because there seemed to be an umbrella-like concoction sticking up from the brown rock. Given that this giant shell was so visually arresting, Davy stopped in the sand and was transfixed by the image.

The lighter brown rock moved and Davy took a step back. The light brown rock was flesh. Davy's eyes adjusted to the image and the brown colored flesh stood up and revealed itself to be a woman. Davy knew this to be a woman because she was naked.

Startled, the woman turned away from Davy and prepared to dive into the sea. She stopped and looked over her right shoulder. She stared and at the young man standing on the shoreline. His eyes seemed bigger than his head. She smiled at him and then dove into the sea.

She was suddenly gone and Davy wanted her to return, but she did not. He decided to return to civilization. The vision of this brown skinned naked woman stayed in his thoughts.

IV
His Prodigal Sheep

It was the baying of the sheep and the barking of a dog that cleared the fog in Davy's head. From up the hill, Davy saw a herd of sheep.

A sheepdog raced around the herd, keeping the sheep from straying. Davy remarked to himself that this sheep dog was one of the best guardians that he had seen in his lifetime.

Davy noticed a tall raven head woman walking with a staff. Despite working in the mud, the woman looked impeccably clean. As the herd progressed to the barn, he noticed a small baby sheep that was slower than the rest.

The sheep dog and the maiden were so forward focused that they missed the straggling sheep. If he were a wolf, this sheep would be easy pickings for Davy. Perhaps, this sheep would be any easy gift for Angus and Jonah. Yet, the sheep looked at Davy and seemed to read his calculating mind. Davy sighed, scooped up the lost sheep in his arms and followed the herd.

As the sheep herded themselves in their pen, the sheepdog turned and barked. The woman turned and saw this stranger with one of her sheep in his arms.

Davy stated, "I believe this little sheep has lost his way."

The woman looked down at her other sheep. The dog continued to bark and the woman said, "Shush."

Davy put the sheep on the ground. The sheep bayed and ran to the maiden. The maiden picked up the sheep and said something inaudible. She then walked the sheep to the pen and gently placed the young one on the ground. The mother sheep approached the prodigal sheep.

The woman continued to look towards the ground. She was trying not to show her tears.

"You're welcome, my shy lassie," Davy said.

She looked up, with the tears on her cheeks and whispered, "Thank you." Her voice was so hushed that Davy could not hear her.

She briefly raised her right hand in a waving gesture. She quickly pulled her hand to her body. Her arm clasped her heart. She quickly turned and tended to her sheep. Davy shrugged and walked back to Angus's pub.

V
His 2nd Night on the Job

As he walked into the tavern, Angus told Davy, "I see ye are on time, I admire that quality in a young man."

Davy said, "I went for a walk. I think I was everywhere and saw everything."

"And you saw the Questing Beast? The blue men of Minch? A Kelpie? Hopefully not a Banshee?!?"

Angus eyes widened with each mention of mythical Scottish monster.

"Actually, I saw two different women. Neither one of them spoke to me," Davy replied.

"Ah ! Women, the most soft and fearsome creatures on the green earth of Latish! Let me guess, one was sheep herder," Angus said.

"Yes, she was taller and cleaner than most women I have seen in the fields," Davy responded.

"That must be Martha. Dear woman, a bit daft in the head, but she cares for her sheep and her crippled papa," Angus said.

"I found one of her lost sheep. She could not say thank you," Davy said.

"I don't know if she has spoken since her mother passed away," Angus said.

Davy felt a twinge of sympathy for Martha. He wanted to help her again.

Jonah asked, "And the other woman?"

Davy shook his head, "I am not certain I saw what I saw. I was looking at some rocks when one of them moved. It was a brown woman, or at least she looked like a woman."

Angus asked, "How do you know it was a woman?"

While his mind was lost in the memory of her, Davy said, "She stood up and she did not have any clothes on at all."

Angus eyes bulged out and Jonah gave his mate a knowing look.

"Not a stitch of clothing at all?" Angus asked.

Davy shook his head and responded, "Naked as Eve."

The three men paused in silence.

Davy broke the silence when he asked, "Do you know who she could be?"

Jonah said, "Brown woman, ye say?

"Brown as the rocks she was laying on. I never saw a women of that color," Davy said.

"A brown woman is not native to these parts, much less a naked brown woman," Angus replied.

Angus looked at Jonah and neither betrayed knowledge.

Davy pondered, "I wonder what she does or where she lives. She jumped into the sea and took nothing with her."

Jonah asked him, "How far did you walk?"

Davy said, "I am not certain. It was north along the shore."

Angus asked Davy, "Did you eat anything before you left?"

"No, just the ale and fish jerky that you gave me last night. Maybe I imagined all this on a tired empty stomach," Davy replied.

Angus replied, "Aye, ye might."

Jonah sat silent.

Angus fed Davy and then put his apprentice to work. The young man managed to fix the chairs that were broken during the Buckner melee. When the Buckner cousins arrived, they did not remember the events of the previous evening. However, whenever they saw Davy, the Buckners looked away. As the evening wore on, the Buckners returned to their rowdy behavior. Yet, when Davy walked near their table, their behavior became very quiet.

Angus commented, "The Buckners are a superstitious lot. You must have made a lasting impression upon them. You did not beat them in the body; you beat them in the mind."

Davy did not understand Angus' comments. He did what he thought was natural. When he herded sheep, he did the same things to wolves that wanted to eat his sheep. Davy established boundaries between himself and his potential enemies. When the boundary was crossed by the enemy, Davy hurt them. Davy's enemies always backed away.

The evening ended quicker than the previous night. Angus and Davy were able to clean up the pub quicker because they had more candlelight. Jonah observed all of this with interest. This Davy Jones had a special quality about him. Angus planned to bolt the door, which was Davy and Jonah's cue to leave.

Jonah said, "Walk me to my home."

Davy said, "Lead the way."

The moon was hidden on this evening. Jonah needed extra candlelight to light his path. The evening was quiet; therefore, every little sound of the night could be heard, from the lapping of the water to the sound of the crickets.

Jonah asked as they arrived at his front door, "So, tell me about this naked woman."

"She was a vision. I am not certain I saw what I saw," Davy said.

"You saw her. She is a Siren of the Sea. She is as capricious and brash as the ocean. There is a touch of destiny about you, Davy," Jonah said, pausing and looking at this young man. "Let your heart not be troubled and may you enjoy your destiny with joy and not sorrow. See you tomorrow."

Jonah limped into his hovel. He waved off Davy with a silent nod good night. The candle faded.,

Davy returned to his windmill and prepared for bed. His body was tired, but his mind was racing with images of a naked brown woman on the rock,

Martha and her lost sheep, Jonah talking about destiny and capriciousness. The sheep bayed with the sounds of the ocean beating upon the shore.

Davy did sleep that night. Yet, his dreams tricked him and made Davy think he was awake all night.

VI
His Daytime Discovery

Davy awoke with wanderlust.

He washed up and walked in the opposite direction from the previous day. The shoreline was flatter and smoother than the previous excursion.

Davy kept looking towards the water, as if hypnotized. He walked into a series of brown wood and jagged rocks. At first he walked past it, but felt himself drawn to rustic site.

Feeling puckish, Davy sat on a big rock and began to eat some fish jerky that Angus provided him. As his belly filled, Dave realized that the petrified wood was once a boat. The boat must have wrecked upon the rocks.

Davy sipped some water from his leather canteen. The boat was the biggest ship that Davy had ever seen in his lifetime.

Feeling rested, Davy rose from his rock and walked to one end of the wooden pile. Davy would later learn that this end of the boat would be called the stern.

Davy observed that there was signage with some Greek symbols on it. The sign was broken with a jagged edge. Davy assumed that the rest of the sign had washed away. From his limited knowledge, he determined that the first three letters were "A.R.G."

He walked around the perimeter of the wreck. There was a mast that was split in two; there were broken logs that used to be oars. The bow was the most damaged. There may have been a statue or carving attached to the bow, but the artwork appeared chewed by some large creature.

Davy stepped over the keel and stood on the sand that used to be the deck. He walked to the base of the mast and noticed a broken box under the mast. Davy kneeled down and looked inside this box. Davy assumed that this box was a safe keeping box, a place for a captain to keep his treasures. With the exception of some broken pieces of wood, the safe was looted long ago.

Davy heard a loud splash that made him look up. The ocean looked placid. Davy looked around and assumed that he was not in danger. He continued his investigation. Davy touched the wood that was placed in the safe. The wood was smooth and shapely. He pulled a piece of wood out. He discovered that the two other pieces of wood were attached to it. Davy pulled out the remaining pieces of wood and looked at them in the sunlight.

Each piece of wood was a wooden statue of a character from folktales he had been told about by the village elder.

With a hand over his face, one figure was male with an arched back. Between the fingers was a stick stuck in the man's face. Davy recognized this statue as the Cyclops, the creature that was blinded by the sailor named Ulysses.

On another carving, Davy observed a feminine figure with a sad expression. At her hips were snarling beasties that were either dogs or wolves or vicious fishes. Davy tried to recall this creature from the saga of Ulysses. He shut his eyes and looked up.

When he opened his eyes he noticed a brown rock in the water, an image he did not recognize from before. Davy looked down at the carving and he made the connection between the rock and a hard place. Davy was holding a carving of Scylla, the lovelorn woman who snatched sailors from their boats while they attempted to cross the maelstrom knows as Charybdis.

The third carving was a simple one; it looked like a prone mangy dog, only the head was slightly raised as if waiting for their master or a morsel of food. Perhaps this was Argo, Ulysses' ill but loyal cur. Argo waited to see his master, Ulysses, when the warrior returned home from Troy.

A loud splash was heard again. This time Davy observed the water. The foam settled and the water became placid. Davy pondered as if he should take these three carvings, for he did not want to be labeled a grave robber.

He looked around the perimeter of the damaged vessel for the remains of sailors who may have gone down in the sea. There were no graves, so Davy could not be considered a grave robber. Davy gathered the carvings and put them in his sack.

As he prepared to walk back to the pub of Angus, Davy looked up and wondered what happened to that large rock that he saw in the sea. The water was placid without a single ripple. Yet, Davy sensed that he was not alone.

If Davy Jones was a bird looking down on this particular shrine of rocks, he would have noticed that the wrecked boat looked like cross bones and the rock looked like a human skull.

VII
His Small Gift

During these long walks, Davy often sang to himself. They were mostly tuneless songs, but with narratives about knights, princess, romance and heroic tales.

Davy decided to visit the mute Martha and her handicapped father. The sheep dog was the first to notice the stranger. Unlike the previous day, the dog's bark was friendlier.

Davy's arrival was later than yesterday; most of the sheep were in the pen.

A crotchety man's voice yelled, "YOU BETTER GET HER HEAD UP! IT WILL SUFFOCATE!"

Davy peaked inside the pen. He observed Martha kneeling over the tail end of a sheep. The crotchety voice belonged to a grey bearded man with a hunchback.

'BE CAREFUL YOU DO NOT BREAK THE CREATURE'S NECK!'"

Martha was entirely focused on the task at hand. Davy was thinking of offering his help, but Martha looked competent. Since he did not want to distract Martha's family, Davy decided leave.

The squeal of the new born sheep made Davy look back. Davy returned to the pen and observed Martha's maternal instincts take over. She wrapped the black sheep in a blanket and sang softy to the creature.

The crooked man in the wooden wheelchair leaned back, resting as if he performed Martha's chore. Davy thought of giving Martha's family a little gift.

Davy untied his knapsack and removed the Argo carving. He said in a soft but clear voice, "Blessings upon your newborn."

Both Martha and her father were startled. The two looked as Davy placed the Argo carving on the half door leading into the pen. Without saying another word, Davy turned and walked away.

VIII
Martha's Hard Life

Davy was late to work, but Angus did not seem to care. Jonah questioned Davy about tardiness. Davy apologized and explained the tale of his day. Davy concluded his story with giving the carving to Martha.

"I'll bet you that old Hephaestus must have growled when he saw you," Jonah said.

"Hephaestus?" Davy asked.

"Martha's Daddy. He was the crookback-looking man," Jonah replied.

"I wonder what Martha's mother saw in that man." Davy said.

Jonah continued, "Hephaestus was not always that way. He was a blacksmith and a good one. He made a suit of armor and lead Scotland's bravest to victory, time after time. Hephaestus warned Baron Von Krutz about the armor's vulnerability, but the Baron dismissed him. While advancing against the Saracens, the Baron had to cross a raging river. Confident in his invulnerability, the Baron forged ahead, slipped on the deck and fell into the raging river. The water quickly flooded his metal suit and he was drowned. The Baron was eventually found in the basin of the Tweed River locked in the jagged rocks."

"This doesn't explain why Hephaestus became a cripple," Davy said.

"Without their invincible leader, the clan lost their bloody battle in chaos. The most brutal and stupid survived, returned home and blamed Hephaestus," Angus said.

"That is not fair!" Davy exclaimed.

"Life is not fair, laddie. The warriors returned from their losing battle and found victory by torturing Hephaestus in front of his young daughter," Jonah said.

"What happened to those brutes?" Davy asked.

"You threw three of them out of the pub two nights ago," Jonah said.

Davy sat down and his shoulders slumped. He had seen these brutal type of people his whole life. Yet, picking on a man for doing his job was horrible. Torturing the father in front of his daughter was abominable.

"What happened to Martha's mother?" Davy asked.

Angus explained, "There must be a special place in Heaven for that woman. Margaret was always sickly, but she brought out the best in Hephaestus.

She had a love of animals and taught little Martha to be a great herder. Martha has a beautiful singing voice and she got that from her momma. Margaret taught Martha not to be prideful; the two would sing some of the most beautiful songs together, when no one was looking."

Angus sighed at the memory and a tear rolled down his cheek. He continued, "Margaret died from shock shortly after watching the Buckner clan brutalizing Hephaestus."

"So, there was no justice reaped upon the Buckner Clan?" Davy asked.

Jonah answered, "The Buckner cousins own the most land. They are like the Hydra, you chop off their head and two more heads appear.

IX
His 3rd Night on the Job

Saturday was a loud night at Angus's pub. Many sailors were on shore leave. After weeks of being cooped up like birds in a cage, these young men would spread their invisible wings with song and ale.

The women of this village, unless they were of a randy sort, bolted their doors. Few women had husbands coming home from the sea, but some had siblings that sought fortune and glory, only to find the drudgery and smell like fish guts and chum.

The most notorious ship to make port that night was the H.M.S. Spider Widow, commanded by the notorious Captain Wagner. Wagner was a charming rogue with a slight resemblance to Jonah. He could charm the bodice off a sister of mercy. Captain Wagner was a fine storyteller and often told stories under the moonlight on the deck of the Spider Widow, or under the roof of Angus' pub.

As much as Angus would complain about the Saturday night destruction of Captain Wagner, Angus was reimbursed for his damages. Angus was also well paid for the information he provided to the Captain of the Spider Widow.

The Buckner Clan was in a boisterous mood this evening. If the Buckner Clan sang a song saluting the monarchy, the sailors sang songs of tales of selfish royal families.

When sober, the song battles began as a friendly rivalry. As more grog was consumed, the songs became off-key and off-color. When the Buckners sang about green wolves and Little Red Riding Hood, which was a slur against the Catholic Church of Scotland; the Black Widow sailors sang about the orange ogres found under the bridge, a slur against the Protestant churches of Ireland.

Neither the Buckner Clan nor the sailors of the Spider Widow were church goers, but each knew that they could insult each other by insulting one's proposed religious beliefs.

Jonah pulled Davy aside and told him, "There will be a fight, a regular donnybrook. My advice to you is to wait until there is a victor, and then knock them out with your chair.

Davy asked, "Why don't we stop the fight before it starts?

"Aye, we could," interjected Jonah, "And miss the show? That would put me out of business."

Davy asked, "Business?"

Jonah nodded.

As the night wore on, the Buckners and the Spider Widow sailors threw food at each other.

Angus commented, "What a waste! That pork gives his life to be on the dinner table tonight. Instead, that pig is being used as a weapon."

Captain Wagner said, "Aye Angus, you know I'll take the roasted pig as food rations. Nothing is wasted on the Spider Widow."

Like the ritual of salmon swimming upstream or the swallows returning to Capistrano, this ritual brawl unfolded as it usually does. Jonah ducked behind the bar and hid behind Angus. Only Captain Wagner leaned against the rail to elbow Davy.

The biggest Buckner lifted two Spider Widow mates in the air and slammed their two heads together. One could actually hear their brains rattle. The Spider Widow sailors then fell to the ground.

Jonah raised his head above the bar rail. After sizing up the situation, Jonah said, "Payday, Davy; go earn your keep!"

Davy looked at Jonah. Angus nodded in agreement. Captain Wagner said to Davy, "Let me see if you can live up to their braggadocio!"

Davy rose from his barstool and walked toward the new king of the mountain. Two of the three cousins who were beaten down two nights ago gleefully waited for retaliation from the biggest member of the Buckner Clan. The hook-nosed Buckner snorted in laughter.

The biggest Buckner stood at seven foot, two inches tall. He growled, snarled and snorted. He roared, "You are in need of a beating, Laddie!"

Davy looked on a nearby table and saw a broken crab claw. Davy noted the sharp end of the claw. Davy looked up at the behemoth Buckner and said in a soft voice, "Your forehead says abuse me."

Failing to intimidate his smaller adversary, the biggest Buckner picked up a chair with one hand and smashed it against the table. Roaring in intimidation, the behemoth charged Davy.

Davy grabbed the crab claw and rammed the pointed tip into Buckner's forehead.

Suddenly, the biggest Buckner pulled up and spun around, turning his back to Davy.

Grabbing two chairs with both hands, Davy slammed the chairs against the behemoth's knees.

The biggest Buckner collapsed.

Davy circled his fallen adversary, who was trying to remove the crab claw from his forehead. Davy felt a pang of sympathy for the felled giant, the same sympathy he felt for a crippled lamb before slaughter.

The biggest Buckner must have sensed this emotional letdown from his foe. The Behemoth grabbed Davy's shirt and pulled on it.

Davy was stunned by the behemoth's gesture, his shirt tightening around his neck. The Buckner pulled Davy closer to his body, intent on strangling his unworthy foe.

Risking his balance, Davy kicked his left leg and aimed it for the biggest Buckner's jaw.

The kick hit the mark, the Buckner giant lost consciousness and fell backward. The back of the behemoth's head hit a tabletop.

The table rose in the air, and then, the table back flipped on the fallen giant Buckner.

The three cousins charged Davy's blind side.

Fortunately for Davy, he heard the stomping of six drunken feet. Davy turned around and pivoted to his side. The three drunken Buckners missed their target and landed on top of the table. Buried under the table was the largest Buckner cousin, who exhaled in a large gasp.

Captain Wagner and Jonah rose from their chairs. The two men smashed the chairs over the heads of the three Buckner cousins.

Captain Wagner then said, "Ye are a good kid, a regular prodigy!"

Davy looked around the tavern and said to anyone who was listening or able to listen, "Look at this mess."

Captain Wagner said, "Old Angus gets compensated when old Captain Wagner visits, don't ye Angus?"

Angus said with a knowing glare, "Aye, yes, but it just gets harder and harder with each visit."

Captain Wagner called, quickly changing the subject, "Let's get down to business."

X
His First Shanghai

Sober sailors from the Spider Widow appeared. An oar was put under the three Buckner's feet and their hands were tied to each oar.

The biggest Buckner was shackled with chains to a wheeled cart. The wheeled cart was linked to the oxen drawn carriage attached from outside the pub. Upon the command of the ox driver, the oxen towed the largest Buckner outside and down the street.

The people of the village sleepily looked out and observed the Buckner bullies being drawn from their village. The excitement was contagious. One villager woke Martha and she told her father the exciting news. Hephaestus eyes radiated joy. He told his only daughter, "Please, go watch. I need to sleep. You need to watch."

Taking her faithful sheep dog, Martha stood on the last hill before the ocean. She observed her tormentors being shanghaied aboard the Spider Widow, a sloppy looking ship so similar the character of Captain Wagner.

Davy felt good about his actions. The Buckners got what they deserved. Martha witnessed the justice her father deserved. At the same time, Angus and Jonas made some money.

The hook-nosed Buckner was the first to regain consciousness and was the first cousin to realize his fate. He was to be a shanghaied sailor who was to be bought or sold as a common slave. The hook-nosed Buckner began to scream and wail when he saw Jonah walking by Captain Wagner and collecting a sack of gold coins.

"Thou art devil, Jonah! I am going to cook and eat your liver! You are going to wish you were never born!"

Captain Wagner told Jonah, "Empty barrels do make the most noise."

The hook-nosed Buckner began to shake, as if he were going to break the bonds of his captivity. Had he been the biggest of the cousins, he might have had a chance. Instead, the hook-nosed Buckner just exhausted himself to the point of blacking out.

Jonah walked over to the prone hook-nosed Buckner and lifted his head by the hair. Jonah then looked at Captain Wagner and asked, "I would love to hear this pig squeal when you brand him. Can you do this task this morning before you depart?"

Captain Wagner said, "You have told me that this clan deserved their fate, and they were a scourge upon the village … then, so be it. This must be the most public shanghai in the history of piracy. So be it."

The crowd had formed on the dock. The Buckners were chained to the mast in a standing position. The branding iron with the symbol of the Spider Widow was inflamed with an orange and red glow. The crowd stood in anticipation. Only Martha and her sheepdog stood away from the crowd. She preferred to remain on her hill.

Davy changed positions several times, before settling on a position where he could see both Martha and the spectacle aboard the Spider Widow.

Captain Wagner began his dark sermon: "In life, we all have a debt to pay, a debt of trespass. These subjects have transgressed beyond trespass."

As Captain Wagner spoke, most of his words were lost to the villagers, most of who were illiterate. Only Angus, Jonah and Davy understood most of Captain Wagner's words. Even then, these three men thought Captain Wagner talked too much.

Captain Wagner said, "Yet justice must be handed out upon these miscreants."

The captain then pulled out a red hot poker. The captain put the hot poker next to the face of the redheaded Buckner. The redheaded Buckner began to perspire profusely, the hook-nosed Buckner began to snivel.

"It is part of the British costume to brand their subjects; some of my colleagues have the letter 'P' branded on their foreheads."

Captain Wagner paused, took a step back and addressed the audience. "Yet," he said, "Captain Wagner of the Spider Widow would not be so cruel."

Moving the poker away from the red-headed Buckner's forehead, the Captain thrust the fiery poker into the hook-nosed Buckner's buttocks. As Jonah had predicted, the hook-nosed Buckner squealed like a piglet. The crowd cheered and laughed.

By noon, the ceremonial branding was complete and the Spider Widow set sail. Davy was tired, but he felt adrenaline from the previous days. He wondered if he would ever need to sleep again for the rest of his life.

Davy observed Martha, who stood like a statue on her hill. Her sheepdog would jump up on her and she would pet her faithful friend. This image of Martha on the hill near the harbor would stay in Davy's memory for all eternity, whether he acknowledged this picture or not.

XI
His Cross Road

Davy spotted movement in the water. It was the brown female that Davy saw three days ago. Like a privileged porpoise of Dionysus, this feminine figure dove in and out of the water. After giving Martha one more glance, Davy walked to the shoreline.

This time, the figure made a point of being seen. She would bob and weave under the water. Yet, when Davy was out of view, she would keep her head above the surface of the water and looked for her voyeuristic friend.

Davy was flirting with her now.

When he was ready, Davy would appear. At first, she was disturbed by the young man's teasing behavior. She was the fish and he was the bait. She was trying to hook the young man and the young man was toying with the fishing line.

No man had been this obstinate with her before. The more she hated this young man, the more attraction she felt for this young mortal. This playful game of cat and mouse continued until she led him to two opposing land masses, the shoreline and an underground lair. At the center of this underground lair was darkness.

She rose slowly from the water and into the remaining beams of light. Davy observed her comfortable nudity, she turned back lowered her chin, smiled and pranced toward the opening of the cave.

Davy stopped and stared. She sensed that she was not being followed, so she stopped and looked back. She stepped backwards to observe this man.

For the first time, Davy felt as if he had two major choices in his life. For all of his life, Davy lived with basic instinct. He figured out what he had to do and he did it. Whether he was herding sheep or fighting the many adversaries who crossed his path.

Following this enchanting woman was different to Davy. He had a strong feeling that if he followed her, his life would be forever changed.

What if he turned his back on this woman?

Davy would live the provincial life that he expected to live. Perhaps, he would develop a companionship with Martha and learn the pub business from Angus. Yet, there was something about this strange dark woman who understood the destiny of Davy Jones.

"HEY!" She called out to him. Davy was jarred out of his thought, perhaps the deepest thought in his life. His vision returned to the siren on the rocks.

With the grace of a swan, she pranced into the mouth of the lair. Davy turned to his left and looked at the ocean. Small waves lapped upon the shore, he had never been part of this water world, yet he felt the salt water calling for his blood.

In his right ear, Davy heard beautiful music. This was music that he had never heard before; it was a chorus of sopranos and altos. The instrumentation lacked the squeak of the bad mandolin and fiddler. This choral music sounded pure.

Davy relaxed and followed the sound of the beautiful music emanating from the lair.

XII
The Vision Speaks

As he approached the entrance of the cave, Davy observed forestation of trees, plants and bushes. He entered the cave.

The soft surface felt refreshing to his sore feet. Much to his surprise, the cave interior was vast and surprisingly, well lit. Along the side of the cave was a series of torches mounted on the cave walls.

A stream of water ran toward the center of the cave. To Davy, this water stream seemed vast, but disappeared at the end of the horizon.

On each side of the current was a series of white basalt steps that led to behemoth pillars and columns. Davy's eyes adjusted to the shapes of the pillars. He was identifying the figures in the stone when a voice interrupted his thought process, "Oh you curious cat," the female voice said.

Davy looked up and saw the figure that he had been pursuing. She stood on the top step and she was dressed in a glowing white robe from radiated particles. The particles of white accented her feminine and exotic form.

Davy's throat felt dry, but he knew he had to say something to this fine feminine form. He thought of saying the cat has no tongue, but then he thought of another land creature instead.

"So who is the spider and who is the fly?" Davy asked.

She was puzzled by this statement, most men in her beautiful allure usually went mute or repeated the same line over and over, "The cat has my tongue."

This young one was a different mortal. She was glad to have put on a dress while speaking in his presence.

"What is your name?" she asked.

Davy replied, "My name is Davy Jones and your name is?"

She said, "Oh, I have many names," and she started to rattle off many seafaring nicknames, which bored him.

Davy interrupted the woman and asked, "And what should I call you?"

The siren was again shocked that this mortal would interrupt her beautiful speaking voice. She would normally smite such a mortal.

Yet, she was extremely perplexed by this mortal's behavior, which made her more attracted to his steely resolve. She thought, just maybe this man could help her in ways she could not even know yet. She had to know something,

"Do you fear death?" she asked.

Davy looked at her and said, "You did not answer my question."

Davy started to walk away.

She quickly walked down to her last step; her face became eye level with his. Her face was vexed; she was always used to getting her own way.

She said, "You can call me Calypso."

Davy responded to Calypso's question; "Death is a part of life. Death is long and life is short. Do not fear death. Love the dead."

Calypso was taken aback. This Davy Jones was a special man. Most men in his position would boast that they feared nothing. Calypso would force them to confront their own personal fear. Frequently, these mortals would run from her cave, screaming like one of Circe's pigs.

The bag under his arm felt suddenly burdensome. With a note of sarcasm in his voice, Davy said, "Oh, fair lady, I bring you not one, but two, boons."

Davy reached inside his bag and produced the carvings of Scylla and the blinded Cyclops. Calypso's eyes widened and she snatched the carvings out of Davy hands. Davy found her actions strange, funny and childlike.

She turned her head and looked at both of these carvings rapidly. She looked at the base of the objects and she muttered a language that Davy was not familiar with. Calypso realized that this mortal was looking at her and grinning. She said, "These pieces will have a place of honor in my domain."

"Domain?" Davy asked.

Calypso smiled her flirty smile, she was starting to feel she was gaining the upper hand in this relationship. She said to Davy, "You have many talents and skills; yet, I see there is much I can teach you."

Davy asked, "You still have not answered my question. What is a domain?"

Calypso said with a touch of annoyance, "Domain, domicile, home -- all different words meaning the same things to me."

After realizing her annoyance upon him, she became coyer with her new prospect. She continued, "You have an attention to detail that I admire. Perhaps, we should talk about the future."

"My future is yet to be written, but it must be a future in which I can learn to live with myself," Davy said.

Calypso said, "I see that you are a man who instinctively helps other people. You have a talent for helping the needs of people. You are truly a guardian. It must be your calling. You went from a sheep herder to a barroom bouncer. I can offer you a better future."

Davy said, "This is the first time I have ever spoken with you. Why should I trust a trickster like you? Who do you think I am? Pan with a Labyrinth? You speak many words, and yet provide no action."

Calypso was speechless, this Davy Jones was the most man she had ever encountered in all of her years. She relaxed herself, but gazed upon his naive eyes. She reached out with her right hand in a cupping gesture.

Davy returned the gesture. Both her hands enveloped his hand, which was rough and calloused.

Her hands were smooth and accepting. This acceptance flowed like a brook towards his right arm. The feeling went across his chest and he gasped for breath.

The calm feeling spread to his heart. His eyes met hers and for the first time since childhood, Davy acknowledged the emotion -- "Fear." As he looked in Calypso's eyes, the fear was channeled into courage.

The passage of time was lost upon the two, one mortal and one immortal. He was at peace; she became complacent, then bored.

Calypso let go of Davy's hands.

Davy inhaled a gush of air and fell to his knees. His heart began to pound in his chest. He forced himself to exhale.

He fell forward and put his right hand in front him to catch his fall. He then looked up at Calypso. She knelt down to cuddle him. He tried to talk, but his words had no thoughtful connection. Only his eyes talked to her.

"You are a mighty man, Davy Jones, perhaps the only man worthy enough to accomplish this immortal task that I ask of you," she said.

XIII
Time to Decide

Davy was on his knees, breathing heavily. He looked at Calypso with incomprehension. She spoke, "Oh, Davy, no mortal has lasted as long as you."

Davy looked at her with awe and disbelief. Calypso read his mind. She gestured to an opposing wall on the cave.

Davy observed two large black circles with white indentions on the wall. Upon closer inspection, the white hieroglyphs depicted two headless skeletons. In the center of these black circles was an entrance to a tunnel.

As Davy gazed upon the tunnel, he realized that the face of the entrance resembled a human skull. Orange and red color light rays beamed from the tunnel entrance. If she were to kill him, so be it, Davy felt he had nothing to lose.

"I deem you worthy to accept this task. You may be mortal, but I deem you to be worthy of an immortal life," she said.

"These big words have no meaning to me, Calypso," said Davy.

"In time, you will understand these and other profound words. Words have meaning, especially my words." Calypso said.

"Despite all that I have read, actions speak louder than words," Davy asked, "What is your barter?"

Calypso launched into her proposition, "In exchange for an immortal life, Davy Jones will accept the responsibility of ferrying the dead to the underworld.

Davy exclaimed, "This sounds too fantastic."

"Yes," she said, "this is fantastic, especially to a mortal. Yet, ye mortals have a limited perspective. Mortals do not think beyond their own myopic vision."

Standing up, Davy said with a note of sarcasm, "More of your big words, Calypso. What actions do you provide behind those words? Or maybe you really don't want me to know?"

With an exasperated sigh, Calypso walked to the entrance of the tunnel. Davy followed and smelled the odor of sulfur. He looked through the smoke and haze and saw darkness.

There was a dim light below Davy and his eyes followed it. Davy's eyes adjusted to his surroundings and he began to recognize concentric shapes of an endless spiral staircase. He could hear water lapping against a sea wall.

"Where does this lead?" Davy asked.

Calypso said, "It leads to the mortal's heart of darkness."

"Why would I want to go there?" he asked.

"If you choose the responsibility that I am offering you, you will learn about ye mortals hearts of darkness, in order to avoid the mistakes of the heart," Calypso replied.

"How do I know that I will get out?" he asked.

"You will be under my protection and you will have a guide, the man you are replacing. His name is Charon," she replied.

Charon the boatman drifted towards the dock that Calypso and Davy stood on. Davy was not aware that he was standing on a dock until Charon the boatman bumped the wooden structure.

Charon was a haggard looking man. He had a beard of grey and his voice sounded ragged. When Charon spoke it was curtly and with one word sentences.

Calypso said, "As you can tell, Charon is weary of his task, I have told him for centuries that I would find him a suitable replacement. You are the most suitable replacement, Davy Jones."

Davy asked, "It will be my choice to accept this responsibility. Was this Charon's choice?"

Calypso said, "Charon was appointed to this position by a higher authority. This higher authority is allowing Charon to exit to the Elysian Fields.

Charon mumbled something like "Go," but Davy could not comprehend.

Calypso whispered into Davy's ear, "I have talked to Charon about his communication skills, or lack of speaking skills, so I have provided you a guide."

Calypso presented a disemboweled head to Davy Jones. The head belted out a howling aria, "My head, my, my hair … OOOOOOOOWWW!"

Calypso said, "Oh, don't be so overly sensitive! Davy, I want to introduce you to Orpheus, your guide to the underworld."

Calypso raised Orpheus to eye level to Davy Jones. Davy said, "Hello."

"Do you think this one can do the job?" Orpheus asked Calypso.

"It will be his decision," Calypso said.

XIV
His Training

Taking Orpheus by the scalp, Davy marched into another dimension of sight, sound, space and time. The concepts had meaning, but with inverted logic of a spiral world with sulfur fumes.

Davy looked back at Calypso. She relaxed against the frame of the tunnel entrance. She waved back and smiled. Calypso's eyes had once again besotted Davy Jones.

Orpheus shouted, "Hey, I can sing you my tale of woe about looking back."

"Is this your first piece of advice that you are giving me in this weird world?" Davy asked.

Orpheus stated, "Heed my words, young man. The Gods gave me glory, but I did not heed their words. They let me rescue my love from the underworld. They told me don't look back. I looked back. Now look at me."

Davy said nothing. Not hearing the word, "No," Orpheus sang about his plight. He compared his plight with that of Lot. Lot was escaping the destruction of Gomorrah, only to look back and see his lovely wife turn into a pillar of salt.

Since he was boarding the boat, Davy failed to acknowledge the Orpheus ballad. Orpheus frowned, shut his eyes and opened his mouth. A ray of light projected from the mouth of Orpheus.

Davy was about to step on Charon's sloop when Orpheus shut his mouth for a moment, turning off the light beam.

Orpheus spoke, "Follow protocol, now, repeat after me, 'Permission to come aboard Captain?'"

Davy Jones echoed the words of Orpheus, "Permission to come aboard, Captain?"

"Erghug," Chiron said, pointing toward his ragged-looking boat, which may have been a mere raft before. It was small and barely contained enough space for two people and much less space for luggage. Charon gestured that he wanted the head of Orpheus. Davy Jones handed Charon the head of Orpheus. Charon abruptly placed the head on the mast of the boat with a plop.

"This will shut this pretty boy up," groaned Charon.

With trepidation, Davy placed his first step upon Charon's boat. Despite being a landlubber of his life, Davy felt grounded on this rickety wood. Davy took his second step and felt comfortable serenity. He looked up toward Calypso, but she was long gone. Davy felt a momentary emptiness until the Charon grunted, "Loosen that line."

Davy did as he was told and the boat drifted away from the dock. Charon reached over to Orpheus and pulled his head slightly back. Charon tapped the cranium and the beam of light radiated from Orpheus' mouth. Orpheus hummed a tuneless song.

The boat swiftly journeyed toward the spiral passage, picking up momentum. The boat began pitch to and fro. Orpheus hummed a different song, a frightful tune. Charon struggled to keep the keel steady, but Davy somehow felt centered and at peace.

XV
Spirals of Inferno

Along with Charon and Orpheus, Davy Jones willingly sailed into Inferno. The flames of the inferno separated the souls imprisoned in their cache of lust, gluttony and greed.

It was as if these souls were posing for a painting, except that these paintings were in motion and they repeated the same hellish activity over and over again.

Davy witnessed two teenagers from Verona who rushed to suicide when they believed that the other lover had died.

Davy witnessed a long-haired man who bullied children and shot a rancher four times in the back. The long-haired man was pulled by a horse by one leg and dragged into the river squealing like a stuck pig.

Orpheus sang, "These rough seas reveal the cost of carnal nature."

Orpheus' singing created a ripple effect upon the waters.

Charon barked, "Will you keep your mouth shut. You will drown us all if I cannot see where I am going."

But Orpheus sang, "Oh, you be quiet, crabby Charon! You and I are both immortal and Davy is the apple of Calypso's eyes."

Charon spat, "Well, I don't want to get wet and I don't want to fall into the blood waters."

"The blood waters?" Davy asked.

"The blood waters are the stream near the violent sinners, those of war and murder," Charon instructed.

Davy said, "So those in war are sentenced to the inferno?"

"Not the soldiers who fight for a heavenly cause. Many a soldier has redeemed their soul when crossing this line. It is the inner voice that one stops listening to during battle. This soldier becomes deaf to the voice and God becomes mute," Charon answered.

Davy said, "God, mute?"

Charon said, "Yes, God provided free will, but God communicates to those who listen. Some turn a deaf ear to God, which makes God mute."

Davy was perplexed and asked, "So you are saying a soul controls God?"

Charon said, "A soul that thinks they control God is truly ignorant to the mystery of life."

Despite the increasing white caps on the ocean, Davy absorbed the words of Charon.

Charon somberly announced, "Blood waters ahead!"

Davy asked, "I saw many sayings at the tunnel entrance. What were the meanings of those words?"

Charon said, "Abandon all hope, ye who enter here."

Davy said, "So, those who enter Inferno are doomed to a life of misery and despair?"

Charon sighed and paused momentarily; after a moment of clear reflection he said, "That is true, but there was one man who did not give up hope and he departed after three days."

Davy said, "Do you remember who that man was?"

Charon said, "I cannot remember his name, but he was a nice guy and a good carpenter."

The rough water settled into a red sludge and the boat slid through the darkness. Davy noticed lumps of cauliflower strewn across the rivers surface. Upon closer inspection, Davy noticed that the dark cauliflower lumps were hairy heads.

"Watch this! " Charon gleefully said.

Charon took some breadcrumbs out of his burlap sack. Revealing a sense of joy for the first time in their encounter, Charon threw the breadcrumbs at the hairy heads. At once, the hairy heads jumped at the crumbs.

The blood water became ruffled and the heads jumped at each other as if they were in frenzy. A bloody arm rose from the middle of the frenzy and attempted to snatch the morsel of food. The arm was attacked and eaten by multiple hairy heads.

"Oh how foul!" Orpheus said.

Charon said, "Stop talking and keep the illumination! Or you are going to be fighting for breadcrumbs!"

Orpheus did as he was told.

Charon pointed out to the blood water and said, "These are the souls of greedy people who used war as profit and denied bread for their own children."

As the boat completed the final spiral of the blood water, Davy noticed that the scene of hellish torture changed. At the first spiral, the torture was man against man, and sometimes a man against machine. If the tortured soul used a catapult in battle, the catapult was slapping back. The soul was treated like a fly being chased by a swatter.

"There was an occultist from San Gimignano who envisioned what we are seeing. Torquemada received his visions from this architect of torture," Charon said.

Charon pointed toward the next set of three spirals. The area was better illuminated than the previous six spirals. Orpheus was able to turn off his illumination and began to sing a song about Jason and his Argonauts.

Davy watched a tall dark figure wearing a flowing cape carrying his own grey head. Charon said, "Meet the Count. He sowed indecision, a promoter of social and domestic separations."

Controlling a smile from creeping upon his lips, Charon said, "Watch what happens to him."

Davy watched the Count cradle his own head to his chest. Upon closer look, Davy observed that he could not see the Count's hands.

A chubby horned devil bounced next to the Count's face. The Count's eyes widened with terror. The chubby horned devil slapped the Count's face and the head rolled away and fell on the floor. A league of devils descended upon the surface; he heard them squabbling over rules with chipmunk sounding voices. Davy heard the Count's cultural voice calling for his body to come find him. It was then that a chubby head devil tooted and the game of soccer began.

Charon got Davy's attention by grunting, "The Count was a gifted man from a royal family. He was trained as a Shaman in a Holy order. He betrayed the order by saying the Holy Order was corrupt. He then founded his own spiritual order.

Charon was interrupted by the bassoon-voiced devil who roared the words "GOAL!!!"

The Count's head then rolled into the net. The body attempted to claim its head, but the body had no hands to grasp. The Count sensed he could not claim his head and that all of his efforts were futile.

Seizing the moment, a cheering devil raised his hands and knocked the Count's head on the floor and the losing devils began to resume their game.

Charon continued, "This Count formed his own separatist faction. His charisma inspired many followers, mostly low class individuals with above average education. He led a revolution, started a civil war and was in secret peace meetings with his arch rival. This Count had a great of deal faith in his abilities, prowess and intellect. His fall grew from his pride."

Charon was distracted by the game for a bit and then continued, "Before creating a public announcement stating the end of war, the arch rival saw a potential threat from a former slave boy. The arch rival requested that the Count eliminate the boy. The Count agreed that this boy posed a threat, so challenged the boy to a duel.

"Despite much injury, the former slave boy was able to cut off the Count's hands. While on his knees, the Count looked upon his victor. The Count's arch rival called for his demise. Obeying a secret agreement between the former slave boy and the soon to be Emperor, the slave boy decapitated the Count."

Orpheus sang, "So the Count is reliving his worst nightmare,
that he is a toy for uncouth Devils.
The Count sowed his seeds of indecision
and grew social and domestic separation."

Davy noticed that the Charon had begun to loosen up; the old man had become instructive. As Charon's mood lightened, the old man accepted the songs and ballads of Orpheus. As the boat descended the spirals of the inferno, Davy started to enjoy the music in the abyss.

As the boat continued on its journey, the torture cells turned into a mosaic of cells stating crimes, sins and punishment that became more convoluted, corrupt and confused. Inverted and perverted, those villains who spread petty evil lived in the bowels of the final spiral.

Charon said, "This is going to be tricky."

Orpheus opened his mouth and let his beam of light shine forward. Davy braced his feet upon the long boat, but made a point of keeping his knees loose.

The boat approached a waterfall. Davy looked at Charon. The boat rushed forward and Charon commanded, "Turn it OFF!"

The beam of white light disappeared. Davy saw darkness with the sound of a repeated thumping. Three lights appeared grouped like three points of a triangle. A white light was on the top, an amber light on the left and a green light on the bottom right.

Davy felt a pull of the amber light. If he were the captain of this vessel, the amber light would have been the direction he would have chosen.

Instead, Charon cut hard to port and pummeled to the green light. A gust of wind and mist engulfed the boat. Davy felt a chill that spread down from his neck to his ankles. Davy Jones swooned.

XVI
Sudden Stop

Davy's first conscious sensation was a happy good morning wake up song, sung by Orpheus. Davy opened his eyes and realized that he was lying face down on a sandy shore. The air smelled sweet of lotus. Davy rose and pivoted into a sitting position. He looked at Charon tending to the boat.

Seeing that Davy was awake, Charon said, "I should have warned you about the sudden stop. You were pitched into the sand."

Davy shook his head and asked, "What did we just witness?"

Charon said, "The last spirals are the wages of sin. As the world grows bigger, hell is expanding. Man had found new ways of harming one another with new machines and technology. There will be a day when one can murder a complete stranger by just pushing a lever."

Davy asked, "So what should I have learned?"

Charon's face registered annoyance and said, "Sometimes, man thinks he is smarter than God, but they never accept the fact that God is always a step ahead of man. Take the Tower of Babel. This tower was said to be created to honor God, but it became an edifice to honor a king's ego. The Tower of Babel was never completed, fell into disrepair and collapsed from neglect."

Davy absorbed all of this information and knowledge. In his former life, he knew that all of these thoughts had nothing to do with his days as a sheep herder. Now, Davy sensed as if this knowledge would help his fulfill his destiny.

XVII
The Smile

Davy stood up and dusted himself off. He looked around and saw a layered mountain. He closed his eyes and took a deep breath noticing that the air smelled fresh and sweeter than he ever experienced before.

Davy turned back and asked Charon, "Is this where we go next?"

Charon said, "Davy, you have another choice. I, Orpheus and Calypso are people of the sea. If you want to walk up the mountain, you will walk away from the sea."

Davy weighed his options. He knew part of him wanted to start climbing the sweet mountain, but another part of him wanted to find Calypso. When Davy looked at the layered mountain, he recalled seeing Martha on her hill with her sheepdog. He was interrupted by the splashing sounds of Calypso swimming in the water. Davy then wondered how Martha and her small family were doing now that the Buckner cousins were shanghaied.

"You look conflicted," a sultry voice said.

Davy turned quickly when he heard the sultry voice. Calypso was in front of him, barefoot walking on the sandy shore. Her eyes twinkled with appreciation.

Davy countered, "I am glad to see you have come to see me. I am not conflicted by that thought."

Calypso blushed and walked towards Davy at a quick pace. She was about to hug her young protégé when Charon chimed, "What are we going to do next? There was a massacre at Macedonia and the souls are starting to pile up."

Calypso expressed annoyance at Charon's interruption. Davy noticed that Charon did not have any empathy toward this moment with Calypso or this sad situation in Macedonia.

Calypso said, "You are charged with this duty and you must fulfill this obligation."

Charon said, "So, Calypso, is this young pup going to take the oar or shall I keep ferrying the souls to the underworld?"

Calypso looked at Davy and said, "This is your choice. Would you like to accept Charon's charge or would you like to return to your pub?"

For the first time in his life, Davy saw two possible futures. One prospect would be a simple, domestic life in the village that would include Martha and the return to sheepherding. Life in the village would provide the family life that Davy missed since his childhood.

The second prospect was eternity with Calypso. It would be full of new experiences, education and adventure. Within hours, Calypso, Charon and Orpheus had shown Davy wonders that he never knew existed, a world scheme that was beyond the grass of Scotland.

Davy made his decision with a smile.

It was not his smile, but the smile of Calypso with her laughing eyes that made Davy want to embrace his future with her.

XVIII
Changing Fate

Captain Charon ferried his boat to the massacre at Macedonia. Davy watched the keel while Orpheus sang a clarion call for the dying souls. The dead and the dying were in the throes of violent emotions. Many of them grabbed the boat and if the boat tipped too far starboard or port, Charon hit the victims with his oar.

Davy watched, taking everything in without comment. He knew he would have to talk to Charon later.

Davy noticed that when Orpheus sang, his soothing songs began calming the most belligerent individual. When the emotion of the situation settled, Charon threw a line into the water and the many victims of the massacre grabbed the line. Charon muttered, "Drowning people, the only ones without pennies on their eyes. I hate cheapskates!"

Charon grumpily escorted these souls to the underworld. By the time they saw the gates of the underworld, the souls let go of the rope and swam willingly to the gates.

Charon looked at Davy and said, "You are starting to anticipate my thoughts. That is not always wise with all people because anticipation is an assumption."

"What do these lost souls anticipate?" Davy asked.

"By the time they reach the gate, these individuals seem to accept their fate," Charon replied.

Davy asked, "Has anybody rebelled or not accepted their fate?"

"If they do, they decide before arriving at the gates. They let go of the rope and they are still wandering about on their own. Eventually, they will accept their fate and look for these gates," Charon said.

Davy asked, "Entering the gates, is that your fate?"

"Entering through these gates is everybody's fate. Some fear them. Some accept them, but nothing matters in the end. We all must pass through the gate," Charon answered.

Charon picked up the oar. With his left hand, Charon swung the oar at Davy's head. Davy reeled to his right.

Davy managed to make himself fall inside the boat. Orpheus stopped singing. Charon looked down upon the stunned Davy Jones who raised his arms in a defensive gesture.

Charon shouted, "YOU CAN NOT CHANGE YOUR FATE! YOU HAVE THE FATE OF ALL MEN! YOU MUST ACCEPT YOUR FATE!"

Davy gained enough lucidity to roll onto his stomach. He pushed himself up as Charon attempted to strike his death blow. The blow landed on Davy's shoulder blade.

Since Charon was off balance, Davy backwards thrust surprised the old oarsman. The two men fell in the boat.

Acting on instinct, Davy head butted his mentor. Since he was the bigger man, Davy managed to subdue Charon by just lying on the old oarsman. Orpheus sang a song of rollicking adventures.

Davy struggled to regain consciousness while Charon trashed underneath him. The frail looking old oarsman forced his elbow over Davy's neck and pressed into his throat. Despite the frail appearance, Charon's forearms were strong from the many years of ferrying souls to the underworld. Unable to reach back to poke Charon in the eye, Davy reached both sides of the boat and began to rock. Orpheus continued his song.

Charon began to realize that Davy was willing to capsize the boat. "No you don't!" Charon screamed with mixture of command and plea.

The boat capsized.

Orpheus held his breath and sank to the bottom of the sea like an anvil. In his panic, Charon clutched Davy tighter as they sank to the depths.

Under the ocean, Charon was at a distinct disadvantage … because Charon was restricting Davy's windpipe, water did not enter Davy's lungs. Charon, on the other hand, fell into the water with an open mouth.

Charon let go of Davy's neck and Davy made his escape. Davy's instinct told him to follow the bubbles to the surface.

Davy saw the boat. With his left hand, Davy instinctively reached the keel of the overturned boat. Once he was above the waterline, Davy started inhaling again.

Davy observed a barnacle, the boat and the souls silently going to the underworld, unconcerned with Davy's situation. Davy gathered his thoughts and said "Calypso."

Charon bolted from under the water and tried to choke Davy again. Charon missed his target but managed to dislodge Davy from the boat. The two fought under and above the waterline much like an anchored buoy.

Neither man had a weapon nor could each man grasp the other's throat. Both men fought to survive while trying to destroy the other. The two drifted towards the shoreline entrance of the underworld. As they drew closer to the shore, a sandbar provided some refuge from the water.

Sensing that he was beginning to lose the battle, Charon grabbed a piece of fire coral and slammed it against Davy's cheek and jaw. The skin tore from his ear to his chin.

Davy fell to his knees. Despite the burning pain in his jaw, Davy realized that he and Charon were on top of a slope on the sandbar. A shadowy claw emerged from the murky slope and sand.

Charon prepared to hit Davy on the opposite side of his face with the fire coral. Charon did not get to inflict his blow.

The crab claw grabbed Charon by the heel and pulled him under. Charon let out a scream. Charon dropped the fire coral. He was totally helpless. The last vision Charon saw was his own blood on the grinding teeth of the crab.

XIX
<u>Arbitrage</u>

Davy pulled himself upon the shore. While not completely out of the water, Davy passed out. He awoke from his deep slumber with the tide coming up and touching his face. Davy heard the voice of Orpheus. He opened his eyes and saw Orpheus lying on his side, apparently he had washed ashore also.

Davy smiled at Orpheus. The smile shot a searing pain through Davy's jaw. He winced and slowly sat up. Davy asked, "What happened?"

"Charon has gone over to the other side. After all the years of grumbling and moaning about the job, Charon did not want to give it up," Calypso answered.

Noticing the cuts on Davy's face, she said, "Oh, my poor Davy."

She walked up to his face and touched his chin. Davy leaned backwards out of reflex.

"You mortals fear pain more than you fear death," Calypso commented.

Davy said through grinding teeth, "I have never hurt like this before."

"Look me in the eye," Calypso commanded.

Davy found this easy to do because her eyes were calm and inviting. He did not realize that her fingers were applying a solvent to his face.

"You may need to grow a beard, my Davy," Calypso said.
"Yes, I may do that, my mistress," Davy said.

Orpheus sang a romantic tune and the sun changed the colors above the land. Sensing that the pain was dissipating, Calypso took Davy by the chin and looked into his relaxed eyes and said, "The world is without a boatman, a boatman to ferry the souls to the underworld."

"That is what I was being trained for, were that not the case?" Davy asked.

"Oh, yes, my Davy, but look how you have suffered already. I would not want you to continue your pain," Calypso answered.

Davy sensed that Calypso was flattering him, for which he replied, "Well perhaps you are right, mistress."

Davy stood up and realized that the water was only up to his ankles, "Please show me the way back to Angus's pub and good luck finding a suitable replacement," he said.

"Oh, ye are a witty one," Calypso stated with her face registering shock, annoyance and admiration.

Davy was one step away from dry land when Calypso began her sales pitch, saying, "You go back to your pub and shanghaied sailors; yes, that is what it is called when you kidnap people and press them into servitude of the sea. You raise those annoying sheep and are at the beckon call of the needy who do not appreciate you."

She continued with her wiles, "Or, you could sail the seas and visit ports of call. You will see wonders beyond the rocky shoals and dirty land you have lived all of your life. You will learn more things and gain knowledge about the weird and wonderful. You will see things you never knew existed in your wildest dreams, but often wondered if any of this really existed."

Davy asked, "But what is the cost of such an honor?"

Charon was so much easier to persuade than this mortal, Calypso thought. Yet, Davy's staunch replies may improve the current situation involving the ferrying of the souls to the underworld.

Calypso replied, "The cost for immortality is 10 years on the seas, one day on land. That is the price."

Davy felt the water on his toes and ankles. The element provided a seductive calm. He closed his eyes and he asked Calypso the question he needed an answer to, "If this was such a great duty, why was Charon so miserable?"

"Charon was old. He performed this task when the world was much smaller. Charon did not adjust and change with the times," Calypso said.

"Like throwing a line in the water and telling the souls to hang on?" Davy asked.

"Precisely, Davy Jones; these souls need to go to their new home. Soon, new land will be discovered and this will lead to more blood sport and blood conquest," Calypso said.

"Charon alluded to your miserly nature," Davy said. Calypso was taken aback by the word 'miserly.'

"Miserly? MISERLY?!? That Charon had a twisted view of the world and he could have had so much more, but he did not ask! He called me …Calypso, Miserly! His fate was too good for him!" Calypso fumed.

"What was his fate?" Davy asked, wondering if the same fate could await him also. "If you are not the miser that you claim to be, what are you offering me to complete this task?"

"I can offer you everything with nothing. What your mind can achieve, I can conceive," Calypso said.

"These souls of the dearly departed are scared and they know nothing of their fate. I want to have a more accommodating vessel. These souls need a comfortable journey to the underworld," Davy stated.

Calypso paused to reflect everything that was just said. She looked at this young man, a creature she could easily smite with a flick of her fingernail at this moment. Yet, this boy had an endearing fire about him. It was obvious that she had besotted him, but Davy had an individual defiance about him. He was not the sycophant that Charon was. Calypso said, "I can offer you everything with nothing."

Davy announced, "That is too cryptic for me, my mistress."

Calypso silently gasped. This fish nibbled the bait, but did not get hooked.

"Immortality is all I can offer and a full day with the goddess. Most men sell their souls for just a glimpse of the goddess," she said.

"As you can tell, I am not like most men," Davy replied.

"NO! You are not! I may be the goddess, but you are more than a goddess. YOU ARE A MAN!" Calypso said.

Davy was shocked by this vulnerability of Calypso; there was innocence in her eyes, a need for him that he had never felt from a woman before. Davy walked up to Calypso and embraced her.

Calming warmth grew from this connection between man and woman and she looked up and into his eyes and grew taller. Davy was looking down into her eyes but now he was looking up, never blinking, the two dissolved into one.

XX
Conception

Calypso's words echoed, "I can offer you everything with nothing and what your mind can achieve, I can conceive. The cost of immortality is 10 years at sea and one day on land with the goddess. This is the price."

Davy awoke.

He was on a boat, floating near the Scottish shoreline. Orpheus was on the bow of the boat. Davy saw Calypso on the shoreline next to the wreckage of the "A.R.G.," where he found the wood carvings that he gave to Calypso and Martha.

Davy observed Calypso, the wrecked A.R.G., the sand and the waves crashing upon the shore. He turned and looked at the silent Orpheus who made an expression that said, "Well, make up your mind."

'I accept with one condition Calypso. That you will wait for me and offer an alternative," Davy declared.

Calypso said, "I accept."

Without hesitation, Davy reached out with his right hand, Orpheus witnessed the transaction.

A vibrant green flash enveloped the three and a fountain of water sprung up from the sea circling Calypso, Orpheus and the new boatman to the underworld, Davy Jones.

All time, space and dimension related to this one moment, merging the goddess and the new immortal man. The immortal Davy Jones issued his first command as Captain,

"You said what my mind can achieve, you can conceive. I would like this wreckage to be my new ship to ferry the dead."

Calypso looked at Davy and smiled. This man was the fresh new replacement this job called for.

"Your wish is my command," she said.

The A.R.G. lurched in the sand, birds flew off the wood and crabs scuttled away from the petrified wood. The ship glided from the sand into the sea. Davy glided Charon's boat towards the A.R.G. With her magic, Calypso abutted the two ships. Calypso said,

"This is no longer the ARG or the Argos, your first duty is to name your ship. Name her well, Captain Jones."

"Perhaps, we should name this boat the Calypso," Davy said.

"No!" Calypso replied, "This is a ship to ferry the dead! Calypso should be a name of a ship that celebrates life, not death!"

"I understand, Calypso," Davy said.

He reached into his coat pocket and felt a hard, oval shaped object. Davy pulled the object, which was attached to a light chain, from his pocket.

"For you," Davy said as he handed the trinket to his love.

Calypso accepted the item and looked down at her hand. It was a locket, shaped like a crab. With grateful eyes, Calypso looked up at Davy and said, "I must reciprocate."

Calypso reached over her head and raised her hair with one hand. With the other hand, she removed a necklace from her neck. Calypso handed her locket to Davy. He looked at the locket, which was strangely identical looking. Davy opened the item and soft music filled his ears.

Calypso pointed to the setting sun, "You will go where I cannot go, but I will wait for you, only you."

Calypso embraced Davy. She looked up at him and shut her eyes; he leaned down and kissed her.

A flash of green intruded upon the amber setting sun. Davy saw his heart protrude from his chest cavity. It was a disconcerting moment for Davy, as he found himself alone on the deck of his ship. She was gone for only a moment, but Davy longed for his Calypso.

The new captain absorbed his new surroundings; his only crew was a head without a body. Davy needed to develop a crew of volunteers, not a shanghaied ship full of captives.

Orpheus alerted his captain about a ship sinking near the coast of Denmark. Using Orpheus as his compass, Davy hoisted his sails toward the Danish coast.

XXI
Progress & Traditions

Davy disliked how Charon callously tossed a line at those poor souls lost at sea. Death could be cruel and the introduction to the afterlife should be a relief from one's pain. Davy encouraged Orpheus to sing a sweeter song to remind people of the sounds of spring.

Davy recounted his shepherding experience; he would recognize the leader and the herd would follow the leader.

Orpheus would sing his song and Davy lowered the gang plank.

"Permission to come aboard sir?" a familiar voice bellowed.

"Permission granted," Captain Jones replied.

Over the keel were the big leather boots, thick legs and the trunk of a burly and bearded man with a bloody face. The new passenger was Captain Wagner of the Spider Widow.

Captain Wagner looked around and said,
"Well, young man, your station in life has greatly improved since your days at Angus' pub."

"Captain Wagner, I am honored to see you again, but not under such dire circumstances," Davy responded.

"Oh yes, I have lost the Spider Widow, but I have enough buried treasures to purchase the Spider Widow II."

Davy realized that Captain Wagner thought that he was still alive. Davy chose his next words very carefully. He said,
"Captain Wagner, my station in life has changed most dramatically. I have replaced Charon. I help souls make their way to the other side."

Captain Wagner looked away. He saw his Spider Widow sinking and his crew swam toward Davy's boat. The Captain of the Spider Widow shook his head, resignation filled his face.

Captain Wagner sighed and said, "Well, young lad, it is my time to sail beyond the sunset. At least I have begun with a familiar and friendly face.

C'mon, let's raise a lantern and salvage my crew."

Davy was surprised at how easily Captain Wagner accepted his own demise. As the crew of the Spider Widow wearily boarded Davy's boat, Captain Wagner greeted each of his crew mates warmly, for some were fearful.

Davy asked, "You do not fear your own death, Captain Wagner?"

"There is a world beyond the sunset and we all must face it. I learned that early in life. I have prepared myself for this eternity. Many aboard the Spider Widow are not so well prepared."

Suddenly, a sound like a pig squealing filled the air. Davy recognized the origin of the sound immediately – it was the shanghaied hook-nosed Buckner cousin. The hook-nosed Buckner kept squealing that he did not deserve to die.

After every lost soul of the Spider Widow boarded the ship of Davy Jones, the Captain called upon Orpheus and the ship set sail. The Spider Widow pirates had never been on a sailing ship that made such speedy knots. The ship seemed to be flying over the white caps.

Captain Wagner commented and questioned,
"Captain Jones, your ship is flying away from the Dutch! Have you got a name for this fine vessel?"

Captain Jones just smiled at Captain Wagner and said,
"You just named her, Captain Wagner."

Captain Wagner was perplexed and asked, "I did?"

Captain Davy Jones looked around his vessel and said, "Yes, this is the Flying Dutchman."

XXII
His New Mentor

As the Flying Dutchman approached the gates of the underworld, Captain Wagner observed Captain Davy Jones. Wagner saw that this young captain was competent. Yet, as time wore on, Captain Wagner knew that the young man would become over extended.

Captain Wagner accepted his fate. He knew that he lived a full life and his soul was what he made of it, good, bad or indifferent. Wagner knew he made his life a game between life and death. He had seen it all and done it all, yet enjoyed the sweeter things in life.

This boy Captain of the Flying Dutchman appeared to only enjoy himself when he was working. Wagner wondered how much company this headless orator would be. He decided to talk to Davy Jones, Captain to Captain.

Captain Wagner started, "Son, you have much talent and ability."

"Coming from you, Captain, that is quite a magnanimous compliment," Captain Jones said.

"Deservedly so, Captain Jones. Yet, for somebody to accept such an eternal responsibility, one must enjoy their life," Captain Wagner said.

Captain Jones pondered for a moment then replied, "Eternal life is its own reward."

"If one can enjoy life, some people suffer even when they have the perfect life. There are so many examples in history, like the pretty boy Greek guy who spends all of eternity staring at his reflection in a pool of water," Captain Wagner said.

"What a waste of time," Captain Jones commented.

"Yes, it is a waste of time, but time is only a measurement. Especially with eternity, time and measurement are meaningless," Captain Wagner said.

"For a man who has not yet visited the underworld, you seem to know much philosophy," Captain Jones said.

"Philosophy is for rich people with too much time on their hands. I have had time to reflect on the open seas. I have regrets. I know I have done wrong things, but I take responsibility for my actions. I pray this might count for something beyond the sunset," Wagner explained.

Captain Wagner looked away and eyes became forlorn for a moment. He wanted to give the young Captain some advice, but he ended up talking about himself. Perhaps, his soul was not as prepared as he thought it was.

"Young man, my point is you have to enjoy everything that is in front of you, because you can lose it all in a small moment," said Wagner.

Wagner started to walk away, absent mindedly patting Orpheus on the head. Orpheus began singing an old Greek dirge. Wagner stood erect, poised and said to Orpheus, "Don't you know another tune besides this old Greek music?"

Orpheus was indignant and said, "There is nothing beside this old Greek music, as you call it!"

Captain Jones looked at Captain Wagner and said, "I could use a change of pace myself, something with a fiddle or horn."

Orpheus proclaimed, "Devil's music!"

Wagner responded, "Orpheus, you have been at your task for so very long that you may have lost sight and stopped hearing the sounds of the world around you. The world of Aeschylus and Euripides has much grown since their days."

Orpheus became silent and shut his eyes. The head without a body said, "I may be eternal, but I am past my time."

A single tear fell down his cheek.

The Flying Dutchman was within a few knots of the underworld and the gatekeeper was amazed to see this magnificent vessel. Even Cerberus the three-headed dog barked his approval.

Captain Wagner observed this and offered Captain Davy Jones a bargain.

Wagner said, "Son, I propose to be your indentured servant for seven years and, in this time, I will share my knowledge of the Seven Seas and the secrets of the ports and harbors."

Captain Jones said, "As the former Captain of the Spider Widow, you would become my servant? Why shouldn't I be concerned that you would become next the Captain of the Flying Dutchman?"

Captain Wagner said, "I did not realize that you were so suspicious for being such a young man. When I was your age, I should have been as suspicious. At my age, I have no desire to command anymore. I do want to pass on my knowledge before I leave this world for good."

Orpheus interrupted, "Don't do it Davy! This pirate will simply betray you!"

"Another suspicious one, with just cause I may add, but my life is forfeit and you two are eternal. I can only hope to make peace with myself. This will be my purgatory," Captain Wagner said.

Davy countered, "A ship cannot serve two masters, but I am intrigued by your offer. Perhaps you can serve as my indentured guest."

Captain Wagner looked upon Captain Davy Jones with admiration and respect.

The Flying Dutchman docked and many souls voluntarily walked through the gates of the underworld. Davy noticed that most souls peacefully accepted their fate. Though, there were those few in line that appeared nervous anticipating an eternity of penance.

The most vocal outrage came from the hooked-nose Buckner whose pig like squeals rivaled the banshee. Ironically, the one labeled the biggest, baddest Buckner easily accepted his fate in the underworld.

"You have accepted me as your indentured guest for seven years; perhaps you can offer the same courtesy to those souls who are not prepared to cross over to the world beyond the sunset?" Captain Wagner inquired.

"Aye, to form a crew of indentured servants, if I was concerned about having one man mutiny, why not a whole crew to overthrow me?" Davy countered.

"Ah, that critical mind will serve you well, Captain Jones," Wagner said,

"Yet, you are immortal. People like me and my crew can only pass through to the next world. Your courtesy will offer a second chance for a lost soul."

Both Davy and Captain Wagner heard the hook-nosed Buckner squeal.

"So, we should offer the most annoying and most obnoxious people a second chance?" Davy asked.

Captain Wagner replied, "Well, I can always practice the use of the cat o' nine tails for the next seven years."

XXIII
His next 7 years at the mast

For the next seven years, Davy Jones and Captain Wagner circumnavigated the globe. The indentured servant purgatory program was a capital idea and Davy Jones developed a fine crew for the Flying Dutchman. As a mortal passing from one world to the next, the voyage aboard the Flying Dutchman became a luxurious orientation.

Captain Wagner was able to reveal his secrets of the Seven Seas. The first secret Captain Wagner revealed were the illusions between man and the sea. In fact, there were more than Seven Seas and that landlubbers never counted beyond their own shoreline.

Orpheus remained disconnected. His songs were ignored or tolerated by the new generation of people lost at sea. One new soul complained, "Oh, great, this is the only music I must hear for all of eternity. I must be going to the inferno!"

In his time and for many ages, Orpheus was the muse of the old gods and conquerors. Now, Orpheus had become a relic of his time. His songs became sadder and sadder.

Captain Wagner saw this as a teachable moment,
"Do you know what is at the heart of a man?
 Understanding one's heart desire can best understand one's motivation."

"Orpheus lost the love of his life and he never got over it," Davy said.

"If we find Orpheus the love of his life, then maybe he can move on to the next world," Wagner said.

"The curse upon Orpheus is eternal from the gods," Davy stated.

"Oh, yes, the gods. You know that his gods and goddesses – Zeus, Poseidon and Aphrodite fell out of power centuries ago? They might be gods, but they were run out of Greece by the Christian people,"
Captain Wagner said.

Davy asked, "So, you are saying that the gods fell out of power and their damnation curse can be lifted?"

Wagner asked, "Davy, what do you and Orpheus have to lose?"

Davy did not share this conversation with Orpheus, but he did keep this thought in the back of his mind for many years.

Between Africa and South America, the Flying Dutchman intercepted a slave vessel that was lost in a hurricane. All of the crew met their demise, including the souls that were chained to the hull of the ship. These chained souls were most accepting of their new world, while the Captain and the crew preferred to stay aboard the Flying Dutchman as an indentured crew.

While scrubbing the toilet holes aboard the Flying Dutchman, the hook-nosed Buckner witnessed the Africans willingly and gleefully accepting their new homeland without any chains. The hook-nosed Buckner said, "Who knew that those darkies had souls? I am glad I am not going to the same place they are going."

"BUCKNER!" Captain Wagner bellowed, "You missed a spot on the poop deck, get back down on ye knees and remove that stain!"

The hook-nosed Buckner looked at Wagner with contempt. Captain Davy Jones witnessed this scenario and later asked his indentured guest about it.

Captain Wagner said, "People like Buckner are fed by hate; hate is exhilarating and seductive at first, but turns into a chip on your shoulder that needs to be placated."

Wagner paused to let Captain reflect upon this instruction.

Captain Wagner continued, "Somewhere on our journey, you will see a white whale. Strapped to the side of the whale is a one-legged man who keeps plunging a harpoon into the white whale for all of eternity. The man's fate is to spend eternity trying to kill this white whale, yet the white whale feels nothing by these puncture wounds. The creature merely searches for plankton on these seas."

While returning to the coast of Scotland, Davy encountered a familiar face, Hephaestus, who appeared happy to see Davy and told him so.

The old blacksmith said, "I am so thankful. Your actions against the Buckner clan made life for us so much better. My Martha is married and about to bring a new life into this world."

Hephaestus smiled wistfully, adding, "I regret not being there for the birth of my grandchild."

Davy also felt wistful; he could have had a normal life with Martha. Yet, Davy felt happy for her, at least he had Calypso waiting for him in a few years.

The hook-nosed Buckner watched Hephaestus disembark from the Flying Dutchman. Hephaestus walked off on his own volition and was not burdened by the shell of his previous emaciated body. The hook-nosed Buckner muttered obscenities about the blacksmith and his family.

The hook-nosed Buckner's myopic anger was interrupted by Captain Davy Jones, "We may be undead. We may be immortal. But as long as you serve under my command as my crew, you will make the head of the Flying Dutchman a clean place. Now, get going or you will be eating your next meal upon the poop deck!"

Captain Davy Jones turned his back on the hook-nosed Buckner, who growled to himself. Davy turned his head and stared at his indentured servant. The indentured servant looked down at the stains and began to feverishly brush the wood of the Flying Dutchman.

Davy was hoping that Hephaestus would look back and see the hook-nosed Buckner swabbing the poop deck of the Flying Dutchman. Hephaestus did not look back, for he embraced his new future.

XXIV
His 9th Year

After seven years, Wagner fulfilled his agreement with Davy and the Flying Dutchman. Both captains benefited from this relationship. Davy gained much knowledge that made running the Flying Dutchman an easier and more fun task. Captain Wagner recovered some of his lost ideals of his past.

Wagner told Davy, "You have been tasked with an awesome responsibility. You are the right man for this job."

With that statement, Captain Wagner shook Davy's right hand. As Davy was about to say thank you, Wagner broke contact, turned abruptly and marched down the gang plank to his foggy new world.

The hook-nosed Buckner witnessed this departure and said out loud, "That figures, Wagner belongs in the sausage land of the darkies."

Davy glared at the hook-nosed Buckner. The hook-nosed Buckner looked down and continued his task, scrubbing the poop deck of the Flying Dutchman.

In the nine years on the deck, Orpheus conversed more with Davy. The songful head had become more melancholy. Davy thought about his conversations with Wagner; he thought about the subject of eternity and faded power of the pagan gods. He began to wonder if Calypso's powers had waned in the past seven years.

In Davy's ninth year of command, a woman in gauze was picked up by the Flying Dutchman. After carefully untying the shroud, the woman was revealed to be Martha. She was still in shock and she kept calling out "Paul! Paul! Paul!"

Davy approached the frantic young woman and put his arm on her shoulder. Martha calmed down as she looked into the eyes of a familiar and friendly face, which had now grown a beard.

She became silent and within a short time, Martha adjusted to her new spiritual situation. She had married a man by the name of McCartney and they sold the sheep farm. Taking the proceeds, the two decided to go to the new land known as the Americas. Despite being pregnant, the husband

and wife found a ship for passage in September. The ship got caught in a hurricane and the violent rocking motion caused Martha to go into early labor. Martha died in childbirth, but learned that she had born a son by the name of Paul. Orpheus seemed keenly interested in this woman.

As the Flying Dutchman headed toward the golden shoals, Davy witnessed something he had not seen since Martha herded sheep, she was singing on the bow of the Flying Dutchman. Orpheus joined in and the two sang a haunting, sad but beautiful duet. The crew of the Flying Dutchman was memorized by this haunting song ... everyone, except the hook-nosed Buckner, who was making fun of the two singers under his breath.

As the Flying Dutchman approached Martha's golden shoals, Davy approached both Orpheus and Martha with a proposition, "Martha, my dear, you have always been my inspiration. Orpheus, the tragic chore you have been made to endure has reached the end."

Both Martha and Orpheus looked at each other and then at Davy. Davy looked at both of them and said, "I propose that when Martha enters the golden gates, she take you with her so you can search for your Eurydice."

"Oh Captain, my Captain, you know I am cursed for all of eternity," Orpheus said.

Davy replied, "The old gods did curse you as such, but when have you seen any of those old gods, Zeus or Poseidon? Who are these gods if they are not mental tricksters? Besides, what is the worst that could happen? You have no body and you are immortal, all the underworld could do is spit you out."

Davy smiled as he said it.

Orpheus contemplated Davy's logic and said, "Why would you want to burden Martha with a responsibility like me?"

Martha said in a soft voice, "Orpheus, I assure you, you will not be a burden to me, and we can learn from each other, while I wait to be reunited with my husband and son Paul."

The three sat silent, letting the profound moment sink in. Davy looked on the golden shoals and saw Hephaestus and his faithful sheep dog standing in front of a crowd. Davy tapped Martha on the shoulder and pointed in the direction of her father.

Martha started to tear up. She rose and hugged Davy. It was a warm and relaxing hug. Martha's touch lacked the electricity that happened when Calypso touched him. This hug was a peaceful easy feeling.

Martha ended the embrace and turned to pick up Orpheus. She raised Orpheus to her eye level and said, "I want you to meet my father."

Orpheus accepted this gesture without argument. Orpheus started to cry as he looked toward his last Captain and winked a goodbye to him. Carrying Orpheus with the care that she would have for any of her young sheep, Martha exited the gang plank and embraced her father. Hephaestus took Orpheus and stepped aside. For the first time in decades, Martha was able to embrace her mother. The sheepdog wagged its tail.

The Flying Dutchman pulled their lines, but Davy stood on the mast and watched the reunion of Martha, Hephaestus and her mom. Orpheus seemed genuinely pleased to be associated with this new family, perhaps now he would find his Eurydice. In less than a year, Davy was to be reunited with the goddess Calypso.

XXV
His Big Day

Captain Davy Jones sat in his cabin. He looked in the mirror and saw a man with a full bushy bear that was groomed several times. It had been 10 years ago to the day that Charon had scarred his face with the fire coral. The beard covered the permanent scars on his face. Davy had almost forgotten about his fight with Charon, for his 10 years upon the mast of the Flying Dutchman had been filled with enough adventures to fill many an old man's soul.

Davy also spent the 10 years modernizing passage to the other world. The modern world was getting smaller and the population was growing geometrically. While Davy knew more than the Seven Seas, he did use the concept of the seven seas to divide the world into seven parts. Each part would be governed by a lord of the sea, mainly in north and south Asia – the Indian, Caspian, Mediterranean seas and the new developments in the West Indies and the Atlantic Ocean. The open communication between Davy and the pirate lords created an efficiency Earth had never known between the mortal world and the underworld.

Davy took pride in a job well done; he looked forward to his wonderful reward, his day with the Goddess Calypso.

The captain walked the deck of the Flying Dutchman. With the exception of the hook-nosed Buckner, the crew of indentured sailors were all new. Buckner still feared his future in the underworld, so he stayed aboard the Flying Dutchman. In front of his captain, Buckner was a compliant sailor, but behind the Captain's back, the hook-nosed Buckner was the voice of dissent.

The Flying Dutchman sailed upon the shores of Scotland. Davy reflected upon his early days of sheep herding, while dreaming about the myths of Perseus and Andromeda.

Davy granted shore leave to his crew. Only the first mate and the hook-nosed Buckner stayed on board. After a quick ride to the shoreline, Davy touched land for the first time in 10 years.

For his first few minutes on land, his legs remained wobbly. His crew began singing, "What do you do with a drunken sailor?"

Davy looked back, smiled and waved. These little moments of humility inspired the crew of the Flying Dutchman.

Captain Davy Jones issued a command – "Remember, we must be on board of the Dutchman before the sunset of the green flash. There are no exceptions."

With a command communicated, the captain of the Flying Dutchman stood tall conveying the strength he was so well known for. Captain Davy Jones said, "Now, you go your way, and I will go mine."

Davy walked along the shoreline and thought about his first encounter with Calypso, naked and prancing across the land.

Today, he saw nothing.

Davy looked around anticipating his Calypso performing a supernatural hide-and-seek with him. He heard the merry noise of his crew, enjoying a hearty laugh. He looked at the waves crashing on the shore. The sound of the shoreline began to drown out the gaiety of the Flying Dutchman crew.

Davy sat down when his legs grew tired. He wondered why Calypso did not arrive quickly to share these beautiful green flowers that were so rare in his hometown. Daylight was burning.

Davy heard a ruffle. He quickly turned his head and looked. He only saw the swaying trees. He rose from the spot and looked at the land in front of him. He decided to step forward.

Davy walked for hours. He remembered walking alone, with only the bees, birds and butterflies as his companions. For the first time in his life, Captain Davy Jones felt anxiety. He thought out loud, "Didn't Calypso know that his time was limited? Perhaps I walked too far." He decided to walk back to the shore.

The land beasts were no longer singing in harmony. The sounds of the birds chirping and bees buzzing drilled his mind. As Davy approached the sea, his anxiety waned and he became peaceful again. A few years ago, Davy had decided to adopt a pet and he chose the Kraken. The Kraken was the last of its kind. It was a cross breed between an octopus and a squid. Davy had rescued the said beastie from a reef in the Florida Keys. It was a stupid creature, but the Kraken was as loyal as a sheepdog. At least the Kraken was a quiet creature.

Davy looked up. He knew it was afternoon because the sun was beginning to set upon the sea. Davy's stomach tightened and, for the first time, he thought Calypso might not see him that day. Davy shook his head and said, "Put that thought out of your mind. Do not allow such wickedness into your thinking."

Davy could hear the crew enjoying themselves and enjoying their one day on land. He spotted a crab crawling along the sand and Davy chased the crab thinking that the creature would lead him to Calypso. The crab scurried under a log. Davy got on his knees and lifted the log calling for his Calypso.

The crab went into a defense posture his claws snapping at Big Davy Jones. Davy gently put the log upon the cornered crab. He sat down and said in a whisper, "Calypso."

Davy felt a pounding in his head. In the distance, he could hear the waves embrace the shore, his crew managing to enjoy themselves, the bees buzzing and the birds chirping. Davy's jaw line began to pinch and his beard felt scruffy and rough. Davy fell back and his body stiffened. He began to press his arms, legs and back into the sand. He said with a whisper, "Where could she be?"

"Captain, upon your word, it is about to be sunset." The second mate said.

Captain Davy Jones said, "No."

"Sir, the green flash will appear. We must make haste," the second mate said.

Davy looked up at his second mate and said, "She is not here. We cannot leave. What if I miss her?"

"Captain, you advised us to depart. We must depart!" the second mate said.

Captain Davy Jones yelled, "NO!" with a sound that silenced the laughter on the shoreline.

His second mate signaled for some crew mates to help them with the prone Captain. One crew mate asked what happened and the second mate replied, "Not certain, this seems to be the work of the devious lotus merchandisers."

The dusk breeze began to envelope the Captain and his crew. The crew began to reach for their captain. When the green flash appeared, the body of Captain Davy Jones began to shake and vibrate. He shouted, "Calypso!"

Davy rolled into the sand and began boring his head into the ground. He looked at the crab under the log, already in his defensive gesture. Davy reached at the crab with his left hand. He grabbed the back of the shell and began to crush the crab.

The crab grabbed the wrist of Davy Jones. Davy roared in defiance. The crab's life ended with a pop, his innards wrapping upon Davy's hand.

Davy watched as his four fingers divided into two digits - then swelled into that of a crustacean claw. Davy whirled around. He knocked a crew mate across the sand with his new claw.

A tentacle rose from under the sea and grasped the crew mate. The crew mate tried to scream but his windpipe was restricted.

The rest of the crew stood there, caught between a rock and a hard place. Davy seized upon the moment. He reached towards the tentacles with his claw. The Captain's body was immediately engulfed by the two tentacles.

With another roar of defiance, Davy used his claw to scissor the four tentacles. Crimson blood splurged upon Davy's beard.

The crew mate gasped for breath. Davy reached out with his right hand to pull the man on the shore.

If the crew mate had use of his windpipe, he would have screamed from the horrible sight. Davy's rescue hand had transformed into an appendage of a slimy tentacle. Davy saw this deformity and collapsed.

XXVI
His Reflection

The pain in his upper left chest woke Davy up. He could hear his heart beating.

He opened his eyes and realized that he was in his own cabin. As he rose from his hammock, Davy gasped for air. His feet were unsteady. Davy reasoned that he had too much time on land and limped toward the swinging mirror.

The image that Davy saw made him close his eyes tight. He opened his eyes slowly. The reflection did not change. The monster he saw in the mirror was he.

"Calypso, you heathen trickster, you have poisoned me with your love," Davy said with a gravelly whisper.

The crew knocked heavily on the cabin door with shouts of,
"Captain, is you all right?"

Davy just staggered away, knocking the mirror and toiletries across the cabin. After stepping over the debris, Davy unhitched the cabin lock. For his first time, Captain Davy Jones saw his mutant crew of the Flying Dutchman.

The crew had transformed into crustacean creatures. Some of the crew was covered in starfish, while some slopped along as jellyfish. The transformation occurred when the crew missed the green flash.

The only ones that did not mutate were the two crewmates that stayed behind, the first mate and the hook-nosed Buckner.

XXVII
His Revelation

The first mate took command of the Flying Dutchman and charted the course to the underworld. He did his best to mask his reaction to the ugliness of the crew. The hook-nosed Buckner cowered for most of the trip, but his curious nature got the better of him. Buckner learned that the monsters had something to do with the Goddess Calypso. He immediately plotted to take advantage of this situation.

The Flying Dutchman arrived at the gates of the underworld. The Captain hailed the dock master and inquired about Calypso's whereabouts. The dock master named Tobey knew nothing. Davy asked for medical attention.

Tobey the dock master replied, "This is the gate to the underworld. Why would we need a place for medical aid? What we got is what we got!"

"I am the Captain of the Flying Dutchman. My crew is sick. Truly, we do not have to live with this affliction?" Davy asked, the tentacles from his beard quivered with anticipation.

"Sir, this is the underworld of the dead. What you got is what you got," Tobey replied.

The lack of concern in Tobey's voice hurt Davy more than he realized. Tobey looked at this pathetic ship master with dead eyed certainty; dead is dead; it is the only constant in the universe. Tobey only knew of only one man, a carpenter, whose death was not permanent.

Davy did not yell, scream or roar, instead he did everything to maintain his outward composure and announced, "Crew, you are dismissed."

His voice was barely above a whisper. The crew began to disembark on the gang plank. The hook-nosed Buckner whispered to the first mate, "So the captain of the Flying Dutchman falls apart because of a mere woman."

Davy Jones heard this and lunged at the hook-nosed Buckner with his left arm, the claw arm. Buckner's head was wedged between the crescents of the claw. Before the hook-nosed Buckner could squeal, Davy bisected Buckner's head from his body. The body went limp as a fountain of blood gushed upward. Buckner's head rolled into the dark water below.

The crew made haste down the gang plank as Davy went berserk on the deck of the Flying Dutchman. The look of terror from the hook-nosed Buckner stayed in his minds' eye.

The mental image switched to that of Calypso laughing. Davy staggered to the bow of the Flying Dutchman. Hanging was the effigy of Calypso. Davy touched the symbol of his lost love.

"Oh, if I could have been made of wood like thee!" Davy cried out.

Davy wanted to be no more.

The pain in his chest thumped like a Japanese drum. His jaw clenched as he grinded his teeth.

Davy made a running stop off the deck of his ship to the gates of the abyss. He was denied.

Tobey instructed, "You must have permission to go further."

Davy shouted, "Get me that permission."

Tobey said, "That is not my job."

Davy roared, "Then, get me your master."

Tobey said, "The master cannot be disturbed."

Davy lunged forward and throttled Tobey. Tobey fought back for a few seconds, but lost consciousness. Davy hauled Tobey over and onto the deck of his ship. Davy marched forward and was met by Cerberus the three headed guardian of Hades. Davy could not pass forward.

The drumming pain in his chest weakened his resolve. Davy Jones yelled to no one in particular, "Damn this weakness!"

The captain staggered across the deck of his ship, where he saw the effigy of Calypso. The pain in his chest drove him to his knees. Davy pulled a knife from his sheath.

Tobey awoke from his blackness to witness the most horrific thing he had ever witnessed in his supernatural lifetime; Davy sliced into his left breast bone and carved into his chest.

The pounding continued and the wound opened. Davy reached into the cavity.

Tobey heard himself screaming as if the sounds were coming from somebody else. This only encouraged Davy as he ripped out his own heart.

Tobey fainted, as Davy held his own heart in his right hand. He said for anyone, "I will feel pain no longer!"

Davy heaved his heart overboard the Flying Dutchman.

Captain Davy Jones stood up and walked to the prone Tobey.

"Welcome to the crew of the Dutchman," he said.

Davy began to unhitch the bow lines when he saw the effigy of Calypso. With a roar of defiance and rage Davy attacked the wooden structure. In his fury, Davy broke the effigy.

With a loud splash, the wooden statue landed in the water and Davy saw the heart wash ashore. Instead of feeling relief, Davy felt a gnawing sensation where his heart used to be. Davy observed another circular object connected to his own heart.

The hook-nosed Buckner was chewing on his heart.

Captain's Epilogue

Nothing, no sound, no touch, no sight.

He told himself that he was a heartless wretch, so his actions were that of methodical thought. Davy Jones had no feelings, unless his heart was near.

Davy concealed his heart away in a chest, a specially-made chest designed by a blacksmith, who happened to be a relative of Martha and Hephaestus. Yet, his heart, which had been concealed in darkness for centuries, had now been in the possession of the British Empire, a worldly empire that knew no sunset.

Arrogant pip squeaks like Captain Sydney lorded over the Captain of the Flying Dutchman. It was like Davy was clearing sheep dung in Scotland again. Davy knew that his fate was held by mere mortal hands. He accepted that premise, but he would make their mortal lives as miserable as possible.

His current crew of scalawags would enjoy Davy's actions against this Captain Sydney. The current crew of the Flying Dutchman was a miserable lot. Misery loves company.

Yet, for a man with no heart, Davy knew he had to perform a sad duty. He had to euthanize his pet, the Kraken. While the admiral of the fleet ordered the termination of the Kraken, Captain Davy Jones considered this a mercy kill.

When sending a pesky trickster to his locker, Davy's beastie was hurt. The tentacles were damaged with open wounds in salt water. The unfeeling creature only felt pain. Davy did not want to let his pet suffer.

The Kraken was the captain's only friend, but he had to let his sole companion go beyond the sunset. At least, the captain would allow this beast to enjoy a feast, the bones of Captain Sydney and the crew.

"Bo'Sun!" Jones called his second in command, "I see a need to send Captain Sydney and his crew ashore."

Davy winked to his Bo'Sun, who understood his Captain's signal. The sun was rising as the Flying Dutchman reached its port of call, which was an abandoned cay near the Northern Florida coast. Captain Sydney and his crew were loaded upon a life boat and launched from the Flying Dutchman.

Davy took particular interest in Pasquale Montalban's behavior. The Roman-nosed sailor whispered something to his pet parrot. The bird flew high and toward the archipelago.

Davy thought, "Did Pasquale have a premonition of his cursed fate?"

As the lifeboat was launched, Captain Sydney yelled at the crew of the Flying Dutchman, "My admiral will hear of this."

Davy replied with a mocking smile, "Yay, that he will." Captain Davy Jones signaled for the Kraken. The lifeboat was half way between the Flying Dutchman and land, when the shadow of the Kraken was spotted.

"Faster, row faster!" Captain Sydney screamed.

Pasquale's parrot flew in a circle around the lifeboat. Pasquale grabbed his rosary and began to softly pray "Ave Maria."

The crew of the Flying Dutchman savored the fear of Captain Sydney and his sailors. Pasquale's quiet behavior held Captain Davy Jones' attention. As the other crew mates screamed in anticipation, Pasquale whispered to himself.

A tentacle raised the lifeboat from the water, but the tentacle was shaky with a tremble. Davy winced as he saw his once ferocious pet in such a vulnerable state.

The sailors jumped off the boat. Only Captain Sydney and Pasquale managed to stay on board. This proved to be a good choice for the captain and his prisoner, for the Kraken pitched the lifeboat to the shore.

The rest of the sailors were engorged into the throat of Davy Jones's locker. Not quite satiated, the Kraken went after Captain Sydney and Pasquale.

Davy watched and hoped his beastie would enjoy one last meal as the tide was going out. The Kraken pursued the two men.

As the two men came within wading distance, both men exited the lifeboat. Pasquale pointed and gestured to the captain to split up. Captain Sydney misinterpreted the gesture and pushed Pasquale towards the Kraken's maw.

Pasquale lost his balance and fell on his stomach, he face dipping under water. He struggled to get to his feet. Pasquale sensed a slimy tentacle rising above him.

Pasquale stumbled again; he turned over and saw his parrot flying around the erect tentacle. The bird squawked. Pasquale observed this and he crawled backward to the sandy shore.

The tentacle fell, creating a loud splash.

Captain Sydney was hit by a wave and fell backwards as Pasquale surged further inland.

Two more slimy and bloody tentacles reached towards some palm trees. The Kraken was pulling itself on the shore.

The parrot circled Pasquale.

A third tentacle circled Pasquale but seemed tentative in touching him, fearing the squawks of the parrot.

The tide was going out.

Captain Davy Jones ordered his crew to keep to the shore as long as possible. He took out his periscope to view the drama unfolding on the beach.

Captain Sydney stood between the two palm trees and felt safe from the crawling Kraken. He viewed the sight of the parrot protecting its master. Captain Sydney said, "Blimey."

It was the last word Captain Sydney said, as Kraken unleashed two tentacles around two palm trees. Coconuts became dislodged and fell upon Captain Sydney's head. Captain Sydney staggered into a healthy suction cup and was quickly pulled in the Kraken's maw.

Captain Davy Jones laughed at the fate of the arrogant Captain Sydney. Even though he had witnessed death and dying for centuries, Davy found amusement when a petty and arrogant man in command received his comeuppance from a poor dumb beastie.

The meal seemed to satisfy the Kraken, which rested on the shore as the tide went out. Pasquale crawled beyond the trees and into the safety. The Kraken seemed ready to sleep. Davy witnessed his sole pet's final moments. He was stoic as he watched his beastie dry out in the sun.

The parrot circled around the dying beastie and landed near the Kraken's eyes. Davy yelled, "Be gone, you devil bird!"

The Kraken raised a quivering tentacle toward its eye. The bird rose and then circled around the tentacle.

The tentacle collapsed upon its own weight.
Pascal's parrot landed upon the tentacle and started cooing.
Davy stopped shouting.

He became speechless as the bird seemed to be singing a song to his beastie.

Unexpectedly, Davy started to tear up, though he would never admit it. His pet, the Kraken was dead and the only creature in this world that showed any mercy was a parrot the Kraken tried to eat.

Pasquale walked out of the forest and beheld the sight before him for several minutes. He then raised his right arm and the parrot flew to his side. Pasquale looked at the Flying Dutchman on the horizon. Pasquale knew that he had to find another way to his beloved Beatrix. He did, but that is another story.

Captain Davy Jones stood on the deck in silence. The festive crew of the Flying Dutchman grew silent and returned to their duties. After he signaled his Bo' Sun to weigh anchor, Davy slowly returned to his cabin in disbelief.

Davy limped into his cabin and surveyed the mementos of his long life. There was a broken chair from the pub of Angus. He used the chair as a club to fell the Big Bad Buckner. Davy lifted the broken chair, which covered a small Aztec treasure chest. As light entered the ark chamber, a muffled scream was heard. With his tentacle shaped hand, Davy raised the head of the hook-nosed Buckner.

"Alas, poor Buckner, you taught me well," Davy said.

The hook-nosed Buckner muffled his pig squeal, as his lips were sown with the wool of a sheep that was owned by Martha McCartney's clan. Davy took delight in the irony of the hook-nosed Buckner's penance.

"When I carved out my heart, you reminded me that I had feelings, so I hid it in such darkness as you are accustomed to."

The hook-nosed Buckner rolled his eyes toward Davy's direction.

I have learned much from you Buckner.   You prefer to wander in the dark, in fear of seeing the light. You are a hateful person, Buckner; yet I know something that is far worse than hate."

Davy dropped the head of the hook-nosed Buckner. Buckner whimpered. Davy turned his back on him and looked out upon the fading island that housed Pasquale and his parrot.

Davy whispered, "People think that hate is the opposite of love; but, there is a fine line between love and hate. Hate is not the opposite of love; apathy is the opposite of love. Apathy is far worse than hate."

Davy became silent.

The blood in the back of his neck pumped profusely. He hated Calypso. The back of his head felt like it was caught in a carpenter's vice. He knew that Calypso thought nothing of him.

Captain Davy Jones leaned over his pipe organ,
too drained to play his dirge.
He looked upon the closed musical locket that he shared with Calypso.
He opened the locket to hear the haunting melody
that was his only comfort.

From the Cave
of
Cinema Dave

The Monkees and Davy Jones

When researching "Davy Jones" on the internet, one must separate the ocean folklore from the featured singer of "The Monkees," the hybrid television show and rock band from the 1960s.

During the waning months of RKO Radio in 1989, Davy Jones visited 105.9 WAXY FM in Fort Lauderdale, Florida (where I worked). Davy was in town promoting the musical *Oliver!*, in which he portrayed Fagin. As a child actor, Davy had played the Artful Dodger.

Davy was a class act; his interview was both funny and insightful. Employees brought album covers and Davy signed everything that was offered. Given the gloom of the impending sale from R.K.O. Radio, Davy's spirit inspired the WAXY FM team that day.

My second meeting with Davy Jones was just as positive. Along with former starlet and current activist for war veterans – Chris Noel, Davy Jones was a special guest for the Cinema Paradiso Beach Party, a special event for the Fort Lauderdale International Film Festival.

Again, Davy Jones was a textbook celebrity - professional, gracious and humorous. My writing colleague, Lena Putzer, peppered Davy with both serious and fun questions. This exchange was captured on the Cinema Dave YouTube channel, titled *Davy Jones and the Mystery of the Universe*. This two minute and 37 second video is one of my most popular videos.

On February 29, 2012, Davy Jones passed away from a sudden heart attack. He had spent the morning riding his favorite horse in Indiantown, Florida. While the world mourned, his memorial was held in private.

To prevent a public sideshow, the surviving Monkees: Mickey Dolenz, Peter Tork and Michael Nesmith did not attend the services. However, the Monkees reunited for a series of tribute concerts, which included the sing-a-long audience participation to "Daydream Believer," the signature song of Davy Jones.

Music critics claim the sing-a-long audience participation is emotionally satisfying moment and a legitimate tribute to Davy Jones. On stage, Mickey Dolenz admitted that this was Michael Nesmith's suggestion.

Grief is a tricky emotional monster. Yet, it is amazing how singing a song can lighten the burden of grief. In a private moment of despair, follow the lead of the Monkees – sing a song. The passing of Davy Jones is not the Monkees legacy. The fun that Davy, Mickey, Peter and Michael provided will be their eternal legacy.

Davy Jones with Chris Noel, circa June 2008, at the Cinema Paradiso Beach Party.

Movies from
Davy Jones' Locker

Decapitations, naked lust, animal cruelty and a fallen hero – these ingredients are not necessarily found in a novella written during the Lenten Season. Following the lead of November's NaNoWriMo (National November Writers Month - in which one commits to completing a 50,000 word novel in 30 days), the story of *Davy Jones & the Heart of Darkness* began on Ash Wednesday and concluded Easter Sunday – 26,000 words and 47 days later.

There is no denying Walt Disney's *Pirates of the Caribbean* influence upon this novella. Screenwriters Ted Elliot, Terry Rossio, Stuart Beattie and Jay Wolpert took the undeveloped legend and created a strong profile for Davy Jones.

Given that Captain Jones and I share the same namesake, I became fascinated by this character. Given that he could be cruel at times, Davy Jones carried a gothic sadness to him that made him more of a monster than a villain, much in the vein of Heathcliff from *Wuthering Heights* or a Marvel Comics villain from *Spider-Man*.

The character of Pasquale Montalban is an archetype character often found in most sea literature, like Ishmael from Herman Melville's *Moby Dick* and Marlowe from Joseph Conrad's *Heart of Darkness*. Usually, these characters are the innocent who listens to the central protagonist, like a Captain Ahab or a Mr. Kurtz, respectively.

Pasquale's surname was chosen as a relationship to Renaud de Montauban (also called Rinaldo Di Montalbano)– a character from the 12th Century European saga about a Knight – Renaud, and his magical horse, Banyard. As with the oral retellings of Romantic Chivalry, Renaud was either a rival or a companion to Orlando, a rebel leader against the tyranny of Emperor Charlemagne. While the ancestry of Montalban and my surname can be debated by academics of genealogy, the character's first name was in honor of a man who made the best pizza pie on Atlantic Boulevard in Pompano Beach, Florida in the 20th century.

When studying William Shakespeare's *Julius Caesar* in 10th grade, our school teacher spent much classroom time discussing how a character flaw resulted in a tragedy of worldly proportions. As much as my public school teachers worshipped Shakespeare, my classmates were bored by the bard's verbose language and the teacher's propensity for over-reciting Shakespearian sonnets.

It is through the musical adaptations of Shakespeare, by composer Giuseppe Verdi, that the effect of tragedy could be truly felt. Unlike Shakespearean actors infatuated with the love of their own voices, a Verdi singer provided some emotional variety before tragedy ensues. In some of Verdi's other works, the consumption of a "female hooker" is made tolerable by the drinking song, *Libiamo ne' lieti calici* from *La Traviata*. Rigoletto's sad fate is made tolerable by his rival's rendition of *La Donna Mobile*. Both alcohol abuse and fickle women is a reliable plot device for the craft of storytelling!

John Wayne made two movies about the sea, *Reap the Wild Wind* and *Wake of the Red Witch*. In *Reap of the Wild Wind,* Wayne is Captain Jack Stuart, a tragic sea captain with a character flaw. In this rare film for the iconic actor, the Duke is bested by foppish Ray Milland and a giant squid in Key West. The Duke is also besotted by beautiful Paulette Goddard in this Cecil B. DeMille epic.

Wake of the Red Witch was released six years later; John Wayne portrayed Captain Ralls, a brutal adventurer at war with industrialist Sidneye, portrayed by Luther Adler. Told with two flashbacks, the audience learns that both Sidneye and Ralls were in love with beautiful, but frail, Angelique (Gail Russell). Between bouts with island natives, corrupt government officials and an octopus guarding a chest of pearls, *Wake of the Red Witch* concludes with a reminder that true love is eternal.

Shot in black and white, *Wake of the Red Witch* forms a nice companion piece to *Reap the Wild Wind.* John Wayne produced *Wake of the Red Witch* and eventually named this his company "Batjac," a strange choice given that it was the corporate name of the company run by his arch rival, Sidneye. Both *Reap the Wild Wind* and *Wake of the Red Witch* were influences in developing the sympathetic character flaw that lead to Davy Jones' personal tragedy.

Based on Jack London's novel of the same name, *The Sea Wolf* has been re-made multiple times in silent films, talkies, made-for-TV movies and as a television series, with tough guy actors like Charles Bronson, Noah Berry,

Thomas Kretschmann portraying Wolf Larsen, the stern captain of "the Ghost."

In 1941, Edward G. Robinson skippered "the Ghost" and shanghaied Ida Lupino and John Garfield. Given the Nazi encroachment of Europe of that time, *The Sea Wolf* played up the parallels between Wolf Larsen with Benito Mussolini and Adolph Hitler.

Produced by Warner Brothers, *The Sea Wolf* was directed by Michael Curtiz, who made Errol Flynn into a swashbuckling icon with movies like *Captain Blood* and *The Sea Hawk*. Whether filming swashbuckling sword fights or bar room brawls in westerns, Curtiz was a specialist in directing action sequences for almost 40 years on the big screen.

Based on the Pulitzer Prize winning novel by Herman Wouk, *The Caine Munity* featured Captain Queeg as a leader in crisis. Humphrey Bogart's breakdown performance was often compared to President Richard Nixon's public fall from power during the Watergate crisis in the 1970s.

While the Captain Queeg's crack-up is the most famous scene, often overlooked in *The Caine Mutiny* are the quiet moments featuring passive aggressive villainy, which became the role model for the hook-nosed Buckner. Upon retrospect and given our perspective of PTSD – Post Traumatic Stress Disorder, *The Caine Munity* concludes with Captain Queeg in a sympathetic light, compared to the bootlicking officers under the captain's command.

In the mid-1970s, Robert Shaw was featured in two of the best movies featuring sea lore, both based on novels written by Peter Benchley. In the classic *Jaws,* Robert Shaw portrayed the cagey Quint, a man with salt water in his veins. A World War II veteran who survived the sinking of the U.S. Indianapolis, Quint's fate brings forth the tragic dimension of destiny - that one's fate is within the stars and not within ourselves.

As Romer Treece in the *The Deep*, Robert Shaw portrayed the hero who mentors both David (Nick Nolte) and Gail (Jacqueline Basset). The three are seeking treasure off the Bermuda reef, but run afoul Henri Cloche (Louis Gossett Jr.) and his henchmen. At least 40 percent of this movie was filmed underwater, with tension rising every time our heroes descend beneath the surface. Jacqueline Bisset was a vision of beauty in this motion picture, even in the scenes without the wet T-shirt.

Ava Gardner's first movie in Technicolor was *Pandora and the Flying Dutchman,* co-starring a young James Mason as the Captain of the Flying Dutchman. With interiors filmed in London Film Studios in Shepperton, seaside exteriors were filmed in six ports of Spain, to full Technicolor glory, circa 1951.

Unlike Davy Jones sentence, Captain Van der Zee (Mason) could set foot on land once every seven years. During his time on land, Van der Zee's goal is to find a bride who is willing to die for him, in order to lift his curse. After centuries of attempted romance, Van der Zee ("of the sea" in Dutch) meets blue-eyed Pandora (Gardner). Will Pandora be the willing bride? Will Captain Van der Zee dance the tango with Pandora?

Three years later, James Mason essayed the role of Captain Nemo in Walt Disney's adaptation of Jules Verne's science fiction classic – *Twenty Thousand Leagues under the Sea.* Mason convincingly presented the didactic psychology of Captain Nemo; an antiwar advocate who has no problem causing the mass destruction of sailors aboard a navy vessel. Given the loyalty of his crew aboard the Nautilus (and their mass suicide), Captain Nemo truly develops the cult of personality.

A lonely Captain Nemo returned in *The Mysterious Island,* a film which featured a giant crab, a giant bee, a giant bird and a giant squid, which was genetically engineered by Captain Nemo himself, this time reincarnated by Herbert Lom. This film is best remembered as a Ray Harryhausen stop motion animation adventure romp.

Sadly, James Mason's last movie dealing with the golden age of sailing was *Yellowbeard,* an all-star comedy that was as jinxed as the Flying Dutchman. Graham Chapman played the title role that featured members from the Monty Python troupe in supporting roles (Eric Idle, John Cleese), Cheech & Chong, Peter Boyle and Marty Feldman, who died during the production of this epic flop.

Yellowbeard, The Pirate Movie, starring Kristy MacNichol, *Pirates,* starring Walter Matthau and directed by Roman Polansky, *Cutthroat Island,* starring Geena Davis and directed by her future ex-husband Renny Harlin, were financial bombs. The word "Pirates" was an anathema to studio executives until Walt Disney decided to make a few movies about their theme park rides, including *Pirates of the Caribbean.*

The Perfect Storm became a surprising hit of the summer of 2000, surprising in the sense that a rousing action-adventure film would end on such a sad note for a summer blockbuster film. Based on Sebastian Junger's nonfiction book of the same name, director Wolfgang Peterson presented authentic New England gothic imagery with thrilling action sequences. While mainstream critics rolled their eyes over the romance between Mark Wahlberg and Diane Lane, tears leaked between the offbeat romance between Rusty Schwimmer and John Hawkes. Especially poignant is the scene where Schwimmer puts on her cheap cosmetics to see her sailor boy off on his fishing expedition, never realizing it would be the last time she would see him.

There have been four versions of *Mutiny on the Bounty*. Matinee idols and poster boys Errol Flynn (1933), Clark Gable (1935), Marlon Brando (1962) and Mel Gibson (1984) have all portrayed the rebellious Fletcher Christian. Charles Laughton created the most memorable Captain Bligh, though Trevor Howard and Anthony Hopkins tried to present Bligh in a sympathetic light.

In the 1962 version, a replica of the HMS Bounty was built. The ship was docked in St. Petersburg, Florida until the mid-1980s. When Ted Turner (a former America's Cup Champion himself in 1977), acquired the MGM Library, he also acquired the 1962 Bounty. Eventually, the vessel was sold to the HMS Bounty Organization LCC, which utilized the boat as a training vessel, a boat to charter and was featured in *Pirates of the Caribbean Dead*

Man's Chest and *Pirates of the Caribbean At World's End,* both films that feature the character of Davy Jones.

On October 29, 2012, the Bounty sank off the North Carolina Coast, a victim of Hurricane Sandy, a Category 2 storm. Despite the U.S. Coast Guard's rescue of 13 survivors, Captain Robin Walbridge went down with his ship. Another victim, Claudene Christian, is rumored to have genetic ties to HMS Bounty mutineer, Fletcher Christian.

Three weeks before the sinking of The Bounty, my Dad – Jerome S. Montalbano – passed away on Columbus Day. This world is a better place today because my Dad was in it. Given that he was first generation Italian American and a model boat builder, it seems appropriate that he departed this world for the New World on Columbus Day.

In his '70s, Dad took up the hobby of model boat building and created three masterpieces, the Vasa (Sweden's Titanic), the Amerigo Vespucci (Italy's flagship) and the U.S. Constitution, the world's oldest commissioned naval vessel afloat.

For a kid born on Long Island and raised in South Florida, hurricanes and bad weather are a fact of life; one learns to respect the legend of Davy Jones' Locker. Yet, in dark times, it is important not to be consumed by one's toxic environment. This was a lesson my Dad instilled in me throughout my life. One has to fight to pursue happiness.

Appendix

Since the publication of *"The Adventures of Cinema Dave in the Florida Motion Picture World"* in December of 2010, print literature had not become extinct. Therefore, here are a list of books that influenced the creation of *Davy Jones & the Heart of Darkness*. As we were cleaning out Dad's closet, I included his books that influenced his boat building craft and the love of the sea & boats. Enjoy!

Allen, Sam   *Wood Finisher's Handbook.* Sterling Publishing Co., Inc. New York. ISBN 0-8069-7914-3   1984

Anderson, Romola & R.C.   *The Sailing Ship Six Thousand Years of History.* Bonanza Books, a division of Crown Publishers, Inc. New York.   1963

Anderson, R.C. *The Rigging of Ships in the Days of Spritsail Topmast.* 1600-1720 Dover Publications, Inc. New York. ISBN 0-486-27960-X   1883, 1994

Ballard, Robert D. with Archbold, Rick McCann, Anna Marguerite (Archaeological and Historical Consultant). *The Lost Wreck of the ISIS.* A Random House/Madison Press Book. Toronto, Ontario Canada. ISBN 0-394-22168-0 1990

Benrey, Ron. *The Complete Idiot's Guide to Writing Christian Fiction.* ALPHA A Member of Penguin Group (USA) Inc. New York. ISBN 978-1-59257-681-4   2007

Biddlecomb, George Captain R.N. Pentecost, Ernest H. Captain R.N.R. *The Art of Rigging.* Dover Publications Inc. New York. ISBN 0-486-26343-6   1925, 1990

Bingham, Fred P. *Practical Yacht Joinery Tools, Techniques, Tips.* International Marine Publishing Company. Camden, Maine. ISBN 0-87742-140-4   1983

Blanchard, Anne Peacock, Irvine (Illustration). *NAVIGATION A 3-Dimensional Exploration*. Orchard Books. New York. ISBN 0-531-05455-1 LC 92-80434 1992

Bradley, Michael. *Guide to the World's Greatest Treasures*. Barnes & Noble New York. IDBN 978-07607-7213-0 2005

Brewington, M.V. *Chesapeake Bay Log Canoes and Bugeyes*. Tidewater Publishers. Centreville, Maryland. ISBN 0-87033-011-X LC 62-18218 1963

Budworth, Geoffrey. *The Ultimate Encyclopedia of Knots & Ropework*. Hermes House 88-89. Blackfriars Road, London. SE1 8HA. Anness Publishing, Ltd. 1999, 2000, 2001, 2002, 2003

Chapelle, Howard I. *BOATBUILDING. A Complete Handbook of Wooden Boat Construction*. W.W. Norton & Company, New York, London. ISBN 0-393-03113-6 1941, 1969

Chapelle, Howard I. *The History of American Sailing Ships*. Bonanza Books. W.W. Norton & Company. New York. 517023326 MCMXXXV

Chapman M.F., Charles F. *Piloting, Seamanship and Small Boat Handling, A Complete Illustrated Course on the Operations of Small Boats Supplements by Hundreds of Problems, Questions and Answers*. 1965-66 Edition Motor Boating, 959 Eighth Avenue, New York, New York. 10019. The Hearst Corporation. 1964

Cianchi, Marco (author), Pedretti, Carlo (Introduction). *Leonardo's Machines*. Becocci Editore. Florence 1984

Cima, Vito Guerrini, Remo Merani, Umberto Muckermann, Astrid Piozzi, Valeriano Telecco, Giovanni (Publishing Commmitee). *The Boat Signed Italy Twenty Centuries of Style* Consornautica 1982

Ciongoli, A. Kenneth and Parini, Jay. *The Story of Italian Immigration Passage to Liberty and the Rebirth of America*. Regan Books, An Imprint of Harper Collins Publishers. New York. ISBN 0-06-008902-4 2002

Coleridge, Samuel Taylor. *The Rime of the Ancient Mariner and Other Poems.* Penguin Books. New York. ISBN 0 14 60.0081 1 1995

Davis, Charles G. *The Ship Model Builder's Assistant.* Dover Publications, Inc. New York. ISBN 0-486-25584-0 1926, 1990

Davis, Charles G. *Ship Models How to Build Them.* Dover Publications, Inc. New York. ISBN 0-486-25170-5 1925, 1953

Douglas, George B., Higgins, Joseph T., et al. *Building Ship Models Patterns and Instructions for a Clipper Ship and a Whaler.* Dover Publications, Inc. Mineola, New York. ISBN 0-486-40215-0 1998

Dressel, Donald. *Planking Techniques for Model Ship Building.* TAB Books, Division of McGraw-Hill. New York, San Francisco, Washington D.C. Auckland, Bogota, Caracas, Lisbon, London, Madrid, Mexico City, Milan Montreal, New Delhi, San Juan, Singapore, Sydney, Tokyo, Toronto. ISBN 0-8306-2868-1 1988

Dyson, John. *COLUMBUS For Gold God and Glory.* A Hodder & Stoughton/Madison Press Book. Kent, London. ISBN 0-340-48794-1 1991

Elliot, Dave; Henderson, C.J.; Leider, R. Allen. *A Field Guide to Monsters.* Metro Books. New York. ISBN 978-1-4351-0530-0 2004, 2008

Field, Van R. *MAYDAY! Shipwrecks, Tragedies & Tales from Long Island's Eastern Shore.* Charleston History Press. Charleston, South Carolina. ISBN 978-1-59629-247-5 2008

Freeman, Gregory. *Sailors to the End The Deadly Fire on the USS Forrestal and the Heroes Who Fought It.* William Morrow. An Imprint of Harper Collins Publishers. New York ISBN 0066212677 2002

Gardner, John. *Classic Small Craft You Can Build.* Mystic Seaport Museum. Mystic, Connecticut. ISBN 0-913372-66-8   1993

Gibbs, Joshamee. *The Pirates Code/guidelines.* Disney Editions. ISBN -13: 978-1-4321-0654-8, ISBN-10: 1-4321-0654-7. New York. 2007

Grimwood, V.R. *AMERICAN SHIP MODELS and How to Build Them.* Bonanza Books. W.W. Norton & Company, Inc. New York. 69-1831 MCMXLII

Hemingway, Ernest. *The Old Man and the Sea.* Scribner. New York, London, Toronto, Sydney. ISBN 978 0 684 80122 3   1952, 1980

Hearn, Chester G. *The Illustrated Directory of the United States Navy* Salamander Books LTD. London. ISBN 1 84065 495 3   2003

Hearn, Chester G.   Friedman, Norman (Foreword) *The Illustrated History of the United States Navy.* Salamander Books, Limited. London. ISBN 1 84065 343 4   2002

Holland, Rupert Sargent   *Historic Ships.* Grosset & Dunlap Publishers MACRAE SMITH COMPNY. New York.   1926

Hubbard, Donald, Commander USN(Ret.) *SHIPS-IN-BOTTLES A Step-by-Step Guide to a Venerable Nautical Craft.* Second Edition, Revised, Updated and Enlarged. Sea Eagle Publishing. Coronado, California. ISBN 0-943665-00-0 1988

Ireland, Bernard *Warships. From Sail to the Nuclear Age.* Hamlyn. London, New York, Sydney, Toronto. ISBN 0 600 39397 6   1978

Johnson, Gene. *Ship Model Building.* Cornell Maritime Press. Centreville, Maryland. ISBN 0-87033-369-0 1943, 1953, 1961

Johnson, Stephen. *The Complete Idiot's Guide to Sunken Ships and Treasures* . Alpha Books. MacMillian USA, Inc. Indianapolis, Indiana. ISBN 0-02-863231-1   2000

Kemp, Peter. *The Oxford Companion to Ships and the Sea.* Oxford University Press. Oxford, New York, Melbourne. ISBN 0-19-282084-2   1976

King, Ross. *Brunelleschi's Dome How a Renaissance Genius Reinvented Architecture.* Walker & Company. New York. ISBN 0-8027-1366-1 2000

Koening, William (Edited by May, S.L.). *Epic Sea Battles.* Chartwell Books Inc., a division of Book Sales Inc. Secaucus, New Jersey. ISBN 0 7064 0445 9   1975

Lankford, Ken. *How to Build First-Rate Ship Models from Kits.* Model Expo Inc. Hollywood, Florida.   1999

Lavery, Brian; Stephens, Simon *SHIP MODELS Their Purpose and Development from 1650 to the Present.* Zwemmer, an imprint of Philip Wilson Publishers Limited London Text and illustrations -- the National Maritime Museum. ISBN 0 302 00654 0   1995

Leaf, Edwin B. *Ship Modeling from Scratch Tips and Techniques for Building Without Kits.* International Marine Camden, Maine. ISBN 0-87742-389-X 1994

Mack, Carol K. and Mack, Dinah. *A Field Guide to Demons, Fairies, Fallen Angels and Other Subversive Spirits.* An Owl Book Henry Holt and Company. New York. ISBN 978-1-4351-1504-0   1998, 2009.

Magoun, F. Alexander. *The FRIGATE CONSTITUTION and Other Historic Ships.* Dover Publications, Inc. New York. ISBN 0-486-25524-7 1987

Martin, J.H. & Bennett. Geoffrey *Pictorial History of SHIPS.* Octopus. London. ISBN 0 7064 0625 7   1977

Martin, Steve. *Shopgirl.* Hyperion, New York. ISBN 07-78768-6658-6
2000

Mastini, Frank. *Ship Modeling Simplified Tips and Techniques for Model Building from Kits.* International Marine. Camden, Maine. ISBN 0-87742-272-9
1990

Miles, Kathryn. *Sunk Outside Magazine.* Pages 79-85, 118-119. April 2013

Miller, Nathan. *U.S. NAVY An Illustrated History.* American Heritage Publishing Co., Inc. Bonanza Books. New York. ISBN 0-517-38597X
1977

Montalbano, Dave (Author); Morgan, Cindy (Introduction). *The Adventures of Cinema Dave in the Florida Motion Picture World.* Xlibris. ISBN 978-1-4500-2397-9, 978-1-4500-2396-2   2010

Norton, Louis Arthur. *Sailor's Folk Art Under Glass.* Old Saltbox Publishing House Inc. Salem, Massachusetts. ISBN 0-9626162-8-4

Payson, Harold "Dynamite."   *Boat Modeling with Dynamite Payson.*
International Marine. Camden, Maine. ISBN 0-87742-983-9   1989

Petersson, Lennarth. *Rigging Period Ship Models A Step-by-Step Guide to the Intricacies of Square-Rig.* Naval Institute Press. Annapolis, Maryland. ISBN 1-55750-970-0   2000

Phillips-Birt, Douglas. *The History of Yachting.* Stein and Day Publishers. New York. ISBN 0-8128-1704-4   1974

Platt, Richard; Chambers, Tina (Photographs). *Eyewitness Books. PIRATE* Alfred A. Knopf. New York. ISBN 0-679-97255-2   1994

Puget, Oliver. *The World's Great Sailing Ships.* Barnes & Noble Books. New York. ISBN 0-7607-0928-9 1998

Roth, Milton. *Ship Modeling from Stem to Stern.* TAB Books, Division of McGraw-Hill, Inc. Summit, PA   ISBN 0-8306-2844-4   1988

Smith, Hervy Garrett. *The Arts of the Sailor Knotting, Splicing and Ropework*. Dover Publications, Inc. New York. ISBN 0-486-26440-8 1953, 1990

Spectre, Peter H.; Larkin, David. *Wooden Ship The Art, History, and Revival of Wooden Boatbuilding*. Houghton Mifflin Company. Boston, London, Melbourne. ISBN 0-395-56692-4 1991

Storm, Rory. *Monster Hunt The Guide to Cryptozoology*. Metro Books. New York. ISBN 978-1-4351-0194-4 2008

Toss, Brian; Shetterly, Robert (Illustrations). *The Rigger's Apprentice*. International Marine Publishing Company. Camden, Maine. ISBN 0-87742-165-X 1984

Underhill, Harold A. A.M.I.E.S. *Plank-On-Frame Models and Seale Masting and Rigging Volume 1 Scale Hull Construction*. Glasgow Brown, Son and Ferguson, LTD Nautical Publishers. 52 Darnley Street, Great Britain. ISBN 0 85174 186 X 1958, 1976

Underhill, Harold A. A.M.I.E.S. *Plank-On-Frame Models and Seale Masting and Rigging Volume II Mastmaking and Rigging*. Glasgow Brown, Son and Ferguson LTD., Nautical Publishers. 52 Darnley Street, Great Britain. ISBN 1960, 1974

Villiers, Alan (Captain) *MEN SHIPS and the SEA*. National Geographic Society. Washington D.C. LC 62-20190 1962

Wainger, Leslie; Howard, Linda (Foreword). *Writing a Romance Novel for Dummies*. Wiley Publishing Inc. Hoboken, NJ ISBN 0-7645-2554-9 2004

Zu Mondfeld, Wolfram. *Historical Ship Models*. Sterling Publishing Co., Inc. New York. ISBN 0-8069-5733-6 1989

Last Call Photos

In the summer of 1975, Dad and I visited The Bounty in Saint Petersburg, Florida, the same ship that sank on October 29, 2012. These are Polaroid pictures that have been lifted from a 38-year-old family photo album.

(Please note the journalistic comments were written by a 12-year-old with learning disabilities).

On the bridge of the Bounty, this is the view that Captain Bligh and Fletcher Christian held (actually actors Trevor Howard and Marlon Brando, respectfully).

Young Cinema Dave prepares to attack Saint Petersburg.

Being a teenager in the late 1930s and 1940s, J.S. (my Dad) and his brother, Paul, were often compared in looks to Errol Flynn. I guess swashbuckling and adventure is in the genetic code of being a Montalbano;

J.S. and I remember the tour guide saying, "This wheel was used in the movie *Wake of the Red Witch*, starring Gail Russell and John Wayne." This picture provides opportunity for further inspection.

Another story ends,
but the adventures continue...

Dear Reader,

Thank you for taking the time to read *Davy Jones and the Heart of Darkness*, I hope you liked it. If you enjoyed reading this book, please tell a friend and/or read my first book, *The Adventures of Cinema Dave in the Florida Motion Picture World*.

As dark as *Davy Jones & the Heart of Darkness* is, this book will conclude on a positive note. This Sea Dog is Chrissy, my best pal from childhood who was named after Christopher Columbus.

Note the spider on Captain Chrissy's cap, which makes her a member of Captain Spider's Yacht Club. Chrissy, Cinema Dave and J.S. (Cinema Dave's Dad) shared many adventures together, but that is another story...

Your pal,

Cinema Dave
Alias
Dave Montalbano
http://cinemadave.livejournal.com

BIOGRAPHIES

Dave Montalbano alias Cinema Dave - Author

A swashbuckling journalist and information scientist, Dave has a master's degree from Florida State University and has lived by the Atlantic Ocean most of his life. He is currently Head of Reference at Broward County Imperial Point Library and The Observer, where he is the longest standing film columnist in Broward County, Florida. *Davy Jones & the Heart of Darkness* is the first of five novels that he intends to publish in the not-to-distant future.

Besides vacationing at traditional ports of call in Long Island, Marblehead and the Keys, Cinema Dave spent the summer of 1996 studying art and literature in Florence, Italy. A Seminoles and a Dolphin fan, Cinema Dave dreams of winning a Rondo Hatton Award. For exercise, Cinema Dave swims, walks and dances at rock concerts.

Rachel Galvin – Illustrator

Ever since she was 4 years old, Rachel has been making drawings. She took art classes in school, but is primarily self-taught. Rachel studied art history in Italy in college. Today, she writes about art for several publications, choosing mass media as her primary creative outlet and career. She continues to dabble in illustrations, whether drawing storyboards for film or illustrating her own projects. This is her first attempt to illustrate a book for someone else. In addition, she is an actress and hosts a radio show, Indie Streak, on which she interviews filmmakers. www.blogtalkradio.com/indiestreak. Find her on Wikipedia, IMDB.com and at www.rachelgalvin.com.

www.ingramcontent.com/pod-product-compliance
Lightning Source LLC
Chambersburg PA
CBHW021113130626
46554CB00002B/675